Rebound

NOVELS BY ERIC WALTERS

Stand Your Ground (STODDART, 1994)

STARS (STODDART, 1996)

Trapped in Ice (PENGUIN, 1997)

Diamonds in the Rough (STODDART, 1998)

Stranded (HARPERCOLLINS, 1998)

War of the Eagles (HARPERCOLLINS, 1998)

The Hydrofoil Mystery (PENGUIN, 1999)

Tiger by the Tail (BEACHHOLME, 1999)

Visions (HARPERCOLLINS, 1999)

Three-On-Three (ORCA, 1999)

The Money Pit Mystery (HARPERCOLLINS, 2000)

The Bully Boys (PENGUIN, 2000)

Caged Eagles (ORCA, 2000)

Rebound

Eric Walters

Stoddart Kids
TORONTO • NEW YORK

Published in Canada in 2000
by Stoddart Kids,
a division of Stoddart Publishing Co. Ltd.
895 Don Mills Road, 400-2 Park Centre Place
Toronto, Canada M3C 1W3
Tel (416) 445-3333 Fax (416) 445-5967
E-mail cservice@genpub.com

Distributed in Canada by
General Distribution Services
325 Humber College Blvd.
Toronto, Canada M9W 7C3
Tel (416) 213-1919 Fax (416) 213-1917
E-mail cservice@genpub.com

Published in the United States in 2001
by Stoddart Kids,
a division of Stoddart Publishing Co. Ltd.
180 Varick Street, 9th Floor
New York, New York 10014
Toll free 1-800-805-1083
E-mail gdsinc@genpub.com

Distributed in the United States by
General Distribution Services, PMB 128
4500 Witmer Industrial Estates
Niagara Falls, New York 14305-1386
Toll free 1-800-805-1083
E-mail gdsinc@genpub.com

04 03 02 01   3 4 5

Canadian Cataloguing in Publication Data

Walters, Eric, 1957–
Rebound

ISBN 0-7737-3303-5 (bound)   ISBN 0-7736-7485-3 (pbk.)

Title.

PS8595.A598R42 2000   jC813'.54   C00-931093-2
PZ7.W34Re 2000

U.S. Cataloging-in-Publication Data
(Library of Congress Standards)

Eric Walters, 1957-
Rebound / Eric Walters.
[262] p. ; cm.
Summary: A young boy who has problems behaving in school, befriends a new boy
in a wheelchair, and together they help each other overcome their problems.
ISBN: 0-7737-3303-5
ISBN: 0-7736-7485-3 (pbk.)
1. Interpersonal conflict in adolescence – Fiction – Juvenile literature.
2. Interpersonal relations in adolescence – Fiction – Juvenile literature.
3. Handicapped teenagers – Fiction – Juvenile literature. I. Title.
813.54 [F] 21   2000

Cover and text design: Tannice Goddard
Cover illustration: Sharif Tarabay

We acknowledge for their financial support of our publishing program the
Government of Canada through the Book Publishing Industry Development
Program (BPIDP), the Canada Council, and the Ontario Arts Council.

Visit Eric's website at www.interlog.com/~ewalters

Printed and bound in Canada

Rebound

Chapter 1

"Hey, Sean!"

I looked up to see Scott running toward me. It figured. I hadn't seen him for almost a month, but he was definitely the last person I wanted to see on the first day of school. I'd even come early because I thought he wouldn't show until the last second before the bell. I waved back weakly.

"How's it going?" he asked.

"Good. How's for you?"

"Terrible! It seems like only yesterday that school ended and we were set free, and now . . . we're back again." He shook his head slowly, looking like he was going to a funeral. Then again, hanging around with Scott often wasn't that much different than going to a funeral — your own.

"Yeah, it's pretty awful," I agreed, although I

was okay about school starting; I just wasn't going to admit that to him. I *was* really glad when last year ended. It had been one long disaster.

"Too bad we couldn't get together more over the summer," Scott said. "Nick and Gavin were wondering where you were, too."

"Bad timing, I guess," I replied. We'd gone to the video arcade a couple of times, and Scott had been over at my house once, all at the beginning of the summer. After that, I'd dodged his calls and made excuses, and then his family went on holidays, and before he got back, my family left on ours. It wasn't that I didn't like Scott — he was fun to hang around with. It was just that when the two of us got together, problems quickly followed.

"We'll have to figure out what we can come up with to make this year interesting," Scott said.

"We'll see," I answered softly. I knew what Scott's idea of interesting was, and I definitely wasn't interested.

Last year we'd managed to get into more trouble than I had in all my previous school years combined. I'd gotten to know our vice-principal, Mr. McCully, a lot better than I ever wanted to. I'd been kicked out of classes a few times, had almost failed one subject, served detention after detention, and was even threatened with a suspension. A suspension! I'll never forget the look in my mom's eyes after McCully had called to tell them how close I was to being suspended. My parents told me how "disappointed" they were in me. I would have preferred it if they'd gotten mad, or yelled, or something, instead of being disappointed. But I guess I even disappointed myself.

It had been a shock for me and my parents. I'd never been in trouble in school before — except for the occasional little thing that anybody who isn't completely lame gets into. My father decided it was almost all the fault of the "new school." I don't really know if that was true or not, but I do know that it takes some sort of idiot to design a school to have nine hundred grade sevens and eights all in one place by themselves. It was like trying to create a problem, and that's exactly what I'd become: a problem.

Sometimes I wish we had never moved. My father had been offered a big promotion, but we had to relocate to the city. And that meant leaving behind our town, the place where I'd been born and raised. My new school had almost as many students as our old town had people. I'd overheard my parents talking about how if they'd have known what was going to happen, my father would have turned down the promotion, and we would have stayed where we were.

Of course, they weren't just talking about me. My older sister, Janice, who is fifteen, seemed to be at war with my parents almost all the time. They were always fighting. The only ones who didn't seem to have any troubles with the move were my twin sisters, Julia and Jamie. I guess life is a lot simpler when you're only four years old.

"This year we rule the school!" Scott said enthusiastically.

"I don't know about that," I answered flatly.

"Of course, we do. The grade eights are all gone, and now we're the big guys."

I was at least grateful for that. The older kids liked picking on the new kids, the grade sevens, and I really didn't like being picked on. More than half my problems were around fighting. That much was the same as in my old school. I've always had a temper, but back home people knew to leave me alone. Here, somebody was always pushing my buttons. And that made me push back — hard. I tried to stop myself, but it was like I just couldn't control it. I'd say something that would lead to something else, and that led to something more physical.

Scott took me by the arm and stopped me from walking. He looked me up and down with a confused look on his face. "Speaking of big guys, have you grown this summer?"

"No, you shrunk," I said, patting him on the top of his head.

"Yeah, right."

Of course, he was right — I was almost two full inches taller, which really hadn't helped my co-ordination very much. I seemed to be spending a lot of time tripping over my feet, which were now two sizes bigger than they were when school had ended. But it was good news as far as basketball was concerned.

That was probably the very worst part of last year. I'd tried out for the basketball team, but didn't make it. Everybody told me that seveners hardly ever made the team, but that didn't make it any easier. I was supposed to make the team. Back in my old school, my safe little school where I never did anything wrong, I was *the* athlete. Here, I was just a big guy who wasn't good enough.

This year would be different. I'd spent hours and hours on the driveway practicing: shooting foul shots, driving the hole, working on my crossover dribble. I was definitely still going to be there after the last cut.

"Do you think we'll be in any of the same classes?" Scott asked.

"I don't know," I said, looking away. I already knew the answer to his question, and I wasn't very good at lying. The only thing that Scott and I would have in common this year was that we were protein-based life forms.

What my parents hadn't blamed on the new school they'd blamed on my new friends. So in an end-of-the-year meeting with me and the vice-principal, it had been arranged that Scott and Nick and Gavin wouldn't be in any of my classes. We wouldn't even eat lunch in the same period.

My friends aren't really bad guys. They are a

lot of laughs, and we always had fun — at least until we were caught. Maybe I should have hung out with somebody else last year, but it was hard to come into a new school partway through the year. Especially a school where it seemed like everybody already knew everybody else. After eating lunch alone for those first few days, I was just so grateful when Scott invited me to sit with him and his other friends.

Maybe I could hang out with them a bit this year . . . we could all stay out of trouble together and . . . no, that was just wishful thinking.

"Come here and have a seat," Scott suggested as we came to the front of the school.

"Maybe we should go inside and put our things in our lockers."

"No way! We have to sit here and be cool. You know, give the new kids a good looking over . . . maybe give somebody a hard time."

"After what happened to us last year?" I asked in amazement.

"*Because* of what happened to us. Last year we *received*. This year we *give*. Haven't you heard it's better to give than receive?" he laughed.

"You're unbelievable," I muttered, shaking my head and starting to walk away.

"Come on, Sean, it's like . . . like . . . tradition."

"Tradition?"

"Yeah. Like Christmas, or Valentine's day, or birthdays. It's just something that has to happen.

Grade eights pick on grade sevens. It's just part of welcoming them to their new school."

"You can just welcome them without me," I said as I kept on walking.

"What's wrong, are you scared that some of them might be too big or too tough for you?" he asked.

I spun around quickly. "I'm not afraid of any . . ." I let the sentence fade away to silence and simply smiled. I wasn't going to go down the same road as last year; he couldn't taunt or dare me into anything I didn't want to do, and I wasn't going to do it to him, either.

Scott laughed. "Okay, okay, we won't do anything to anybody . . . at least for today. My mom would kill me if I got in trouble on day one. Just come and have a seat with me, and we'll have a last couple of breaths of fresh air. Okay?" He patted a spot on the ramp beside him.

I hesitated.

"Come on, what harm could it do?"

He was right. What harm could it do to just sit with him for a few minutes? I nodded and plopped down beside him.

This was the very best place to watch everybody go up the stairs into the school. It was also the spot that was "owned" by the cool grade eights — a spot where I wouldn't sit on a bet last year.

As we sat there, a trickle of kids began to flow

past. Cars pulled into the driveway of the school and kids jumped out. Even if I didn't know all the grade eights, it was obvious which were the new kids. They mostly had a look of confusion, or fear, or wonderment, like they were entering Disney World instead of Homelands Senior Public School.

As kids went by, Scott leaned closer to me and quietly made funny comments. He always did crack me up and I tried to stifle my laughter. I'd missed hanging with him. Maybe things could be different this year . . . maybe he wanted to stay out of trouble, too . . . maybe we could spend some time together.

"Those are some shoes," Scott said, pointing down at my feet.

I smiled and pulled one of my feet up onto the ramp beside me. "They're the best there is."

I was pleased he'd noticed. They were the most expensive shoes Nike made, and it had taken me a long time to convince my parents that I needed them. My father loved basketball, but he said it was still hard to spend more money for a pair of shoes than it cost for his first car.

"Are you trying out for the basketball team?" Scott asked.

"Not trying out. Making it."

"That's the attitude." He paused, and a sinister smile crept onto his face. "Then I guess you don't want one of these," he said, pulling out a package of cigarettes.

"Of course not!"

He took a cigarette out of the package and put it in his mouth. From his other pocket he produced a lighter and flicked it.

"Are you crazy?" I asked. "You can't smoke on the front steps of the school!"

"I can't during the school year, but the year doesn't start for another . . ." he turned his wrist over and looked at his watch, ". . . twenty-two minutes."

"It doesn't work like that. You smoke here and they'll suspend you. Besides, since when did you smoke?"

"I've smoked for a long time. Almost three weeks."

Besides being expensive and causing cancer, it wasn't good for your lungs. I needed all my air for sports.

"What made you start smoking?" I asked.

"You know, all the reasons from that movie we saw in Health last year. Peer pressure, advertising, trying to look cool, impressing people."

"Then it's working," I said. "You've impressed me."

"I have?" Scott said, looking pleased with himself.

"Yeah, you've impressed me that you're an even bigger idiot than I thought you were."

Scott chuckled. Knowing Scott, I think he took

that as a compliment.

"Well, if you're not going to smoke, you're going to have to do something to keep up with me. How about getting one of these?" Scott suggested as he opened his mouth and stuck out his tongue.

There in the middle of his tongue was a shiny metal stud.

"You didn't!" I exclaimed.

"Do you like it?" he asked.

"I just can't believe you did it. That must have hurt something bad."

"It did. Piercing isn't for wimps. So what do you think?"

"I was just thinking that if there was anybody in the whole world who didn't need another hole in his head, it's you."

"I'll give *you* another hole in the head!" Scott threatened. He reached out to take a poke at me, but only caught empty air as I jumped up and out of the way. I smiled smugly.

Suddenly I was pushed strongly from behind and was almost knocked off my feet.

"Hey, what's the idea you . . ." My sentence faded into nothing as my mouth hung open. I looked down at a kid in a wheelchair.

"The idea is you should watch where you're going," he said loudly.

I stared at him. He had frosted hair, an earring, and was wearing a hockey jersey. I'd never seen him before, but he didn't look like some scared sevener.

"Are you going to move or just stand there and look stupid?" he asked.

"What?" I asked, dumbfounded.

"Those were all little words. What didn't you understand?"

I heard a twittering of laughter and looked over my shoulder. A knot of kids had stopped on the steps and were watching. I felt the hairs on the back of my neck start to stand on end . . . I didn't like being laughed at.

"Hey!" I screamed as the chair bumped into me again.

"Either get wheels or get off the ramp!"

There was more laughter from behind. I was being made to look like a fool in front of all these kids by some guy in a wheelchair. This wasn't how the first day of school — my new beginning — was supposed to start. This wasn't real.

"This is your last warning. Either you move or I make you move."

I felt myself snap. "I'd like to see you try," I growled. I planted my feet and my hands curled into fists.

"Sean, what are you doing, man . . . the guy's in a wheelchair," Scott said.

I looked at Scott and then at the crowd of people standing and gawking. There was silence. On a number of faces I could see the same look of amazement that Scott wore. What kind of guy gets into a fight with somebody in a wheelchair?

I uncurled my fingers and turned back to the boy and gave him a half-smile. Then I looked over at Scott and shrugged. Amazingly, he had just saved me from getting into trouble. Maybe despite the smokes and tongue stud, Scott might just —

"Last chance," the kid said.

"What?"

"Those were small words, too."

"I was just — oooofffffff!" All the air rushed out of my lungs, and pain shot up into my brain. I'd been punched! Before I could react, a second blow hit me lower and I doubled over. I reached up to ward off the next blow, but staggered, lost my balance, and fell forward, landing on top of him in the chair. My eyes teared, and all I could hear were his curses and the collective gasps and screams of the crowd surrounding us. Despite my weight pinning him beneath me, he still was trying to strike me! I tied his arms up in mine but didn't have the power to push off or strike back. It took all my strength just to keep his arms locked under mine, and he struggled wildly to get one free. I had to hold on.

All at once, I became aware that we were moving, backward, down the wheelchair ramp, picking up speed. I tried to get off the chair, but we were so tangled together I couldn't get free! With a heavy bump we hit the end, and I felt myself going head over heels, somersaulting through the air with this kid still wrapped in my arms. We crashed down heavily into the pavement and skidded along the surface, still tied together in one ball. I freed up an arm and instantly another punch rained down on me, bouncing off the top of my head. In desperation, I reached forward and grabbed him again.

"What's going on here?" I heard a voice bark out.

Chapter 2

I knew that voice . . . I still heard it in my dreams
— or, really, my nightmares. It was our vice-
principal, Mr. McCully.

Somehow I had to get away, melt into the
crowd. I was dead if he found me rolling around on
the ground. I had to get free — fast! I tried to dis-
entangle myself and was stunned by another shot
to the side of the head. What was he doing? We
had to get away. My fear of getting caught far
outweighed the sting of the blow. Desperately, I
pushed off against him, shoving him backward,
and crawled away. I knew I wouldn't have to get
far to get away from another hit — after all, it
wasn't like he could chase me. I bashed into the
legs of somebody, and, before I could even think,
I was pulled to my feet. I looked up. Mr. McCully

was holding onto me.

"What do you think you're doing, McGregor?" he demanded loudly.

He always called people by their last names when he was mad. I don't think he even knew my first name.

"What's going on?" he demanded again.

What could I say? What I was doing and what it looked like were two different things.

"Get to my office! You *know* where it is!"

"But . . . but . . ." I stammered. No matter what he thought, I was the innocent victim!

"No buts! Get to my office — now!" he yelled. He turned to the other kid. "And you," he said, pointing a finger at him, "get to your feet, immediately!"

"Can't do that unless you got an extra set of legs on you."

Mr. McCully looked momentarily stunned by his answer, but then he gave the kid his customary angry glare.

"I don't know who you are, but at this school you'd better learn to listen to your teachers and do what you're . . ." His voice trailed off as he watched the kid drag himself over to his chair, tip it onto its wheels, pull himself up, and settle back into the seat. The look on McCully's face was total and complete shock.

"Are you all right, son?" he asked as he rushed over to his side. I heard him say something, but couldn't make out what it was. Satisfied, Mr. McCully turned around and came back toward me. I was frightened by the look in his eyes and stumbled back a couple of steps. I'd seen him mad before — more than a few times — but I'd never seen him look like this. I felt a rush of fear.

"Didn't I tell you to get to my office!"

"Yeah, I was just —"

"Right now!" He spat out the words as he grabbed me by the arm and started to drag me away from the crowd. His fingers dug into my arm, but I didn't care. Kids parted to let us pass. It looked like half the school was standing around watching. I knew that anybody who wasn't here would hear about it before the end of first period.

My left elbow was aching from where I'd hit the ground, and I could see the knuckles of that hand were scraped and bleeding.

"This is a new low, even for you," Mr. McCully hissed through clenched teeth.

"You don't understand!" I protested.

"I understand too well. You couldn't even last until the first bell on the first day before you picked a fight."

"I wasn't fighting."

"I saw it with my own eyes so don't even try to lie your way out of it! And with a kid in a wheelchair . . . unbelievable . . ." He let go of me as we entered his office. "Sit down," he ordered.

I settled into my familiar chair right in front of

his desk. Some of the worst moments of my whole life were spent sitting in this chair.

"What were you thinking?" he demanded. "All those promises you made to me and your parents at the end of the year were completely worthless."

They weren't worthless . . . I really meant every word I said . . . I was going to stay out of trouble . . .

"What do you think your parents are going to say when I call them?"

Oh my goodness . . . I knew what they were going to say. But it was what they were going to *do* that scared me. Grounded I could handle, but would they forbid me to play ball?

"Couldn't you just give me another chance?" I pleaded.

"You ran out of chances last year."

"Do my parents really have to hear about it? I served detentions last year where you didn't call them. Please!"

"I have to call them. A phone call is necessary when a student is suspended from school."

"Suspended!" I gasped.

"Yes."

"But you can't suspend me!"

"Of course, I can, I'm the vice-principal."

"But you didn't suspend me for fighting last year."

"I guess I should have done it before, but I thought most of those fights weren't your fault."

"They weren't — and neither was this one!"

"Don't play me for an idiot, McGregor. Are you trying to tell me that a boy in a wheelchair, for no reason, was picking on *you*?"

"That's how it happened. He started it." That didn't even sound believable to me.

"You're saying he struck you first?" he asked in an incredulous tone.

"First and second and third and last. I didn't hit him at all!" I answered emphatically.

"I saw you wrestling with him, rolling around on the ground."

"He hit me and I fell on him and the chair rolled down the ramp."

"And how do you explain your bleeding knuckles?" he asked, pointing to my injured hand.

"That happened when we got thrown to the ground and —"

"Enough!" he said, cutting me off. "I don't want to hear another word. Just sit there while I call your parents."

"But it wasn't my fault, honestly! Couldn't you just ask somebody what happened? Scott was right beside me when the kid started it."

"Right, I'm going to believe Scott," he huffed. "You two spent half of last year covering for each other."

"Ask anybody. Half the school must have seen!" Seen me get insulted and hit by a wheelchair kid. "Just talk to somebody, anybody, before you call my parents. That's all I'm asking," I pleaded.

"There's no point in delaying the inevitable. You're going to be suspended."

"But that's not fair!" I protested.

"And was it fair for you to be fighting with a student who's in a wheelchair?"

"I wasn't fighting and —"

He put up his hand to silence me.

"And . . . I was just hoping you could talk to people . . . investigate . . . you know, innocent until proven guilty? What happened to the fresh start you promised me?" I asked.

For the first time his expression softened — not much, but a little — until he looked only really angry. "Is that the same conversation where you said you wouldn't get in any more fights?" he asked.

I slowly nodded my head. "I wasn't fighting. If you asked some people and if they didn't see it that way, then I'll just shut up . . . you can suspend me."

He rose from his seat. "Wait outside and I'll conduct an investigation."

"Thank you!" I said as I rose to my feet as well.

"Don't thank me yet. I might just be gathering more evidence to make the suspension longer." He motioned to the door and I left his office.

I walked over to the drinking fountain and took a long drink. It felt good — my mouth was as dry as cotton. Next I put my hand in the stream of water. It stung slightly as the water washed away the blood. I shook off the excess water and then dried my hand on the side of my pants. At least my pants were still intact. Ripping my back-to-school clothes would have been the final nail in my coffin.

I walked over and took a seat on the bench on the wall outside the office. This seat was even more familiar to me than the spot in Mr. McCully's office. This is where you sat before and after dealing with the vice-principal. And, in some ways, it was an even worse spot to be than in his office. At least in there you had some privacy. Here you were on public display as people moved through the halls. Mostly they didn't even make eye contact with you, but everybody who went by knew you weren't sitting there waiting for a bus.

This was the spot where I'd first met Scott last year, before he invited me to sit with him at lunch. I'd seen him on the bench a couple of times before I was ever sent there myself. I remember thinking "poor sucker." And that's how I felt that first time I did some bench time. Then Scott showed up and he sat down beside me and started joking around and he made me feel less awful. There's no question that's when we became friends.

As the year went on I had more practice sitting out here on the bench. Scott was with me most of the time and that helped. He'd make us laugh, talk to people who were passing by. Sometimes it felt like he almost enjoyed being there.

I took a deep breath. No matter how Scott felt, I didn't like being here. I kept my eyes on the ground so all I could see were feet trudging by. Hopefully, I wouldn't be here for long. Soon this would all be cleared up; people would tell him what really happened. I turned the whole thing over in my mind again. I was there, it happened to me, and I hardly believed it. But suddenly it struck me. What if they'd seen it wrong, or come at the end when we were rolling around? Or what if their view was blocked and they only saw me fall on him, not those first punches that made me fall? Or what if they only remembered me from getting in fights last year? I knew I couldn't be certain what people had seen or what they thought they saw. I slumped forward and buried my face in my hands. I wanted so badly for this year to start off on the right foot and now I felt like I was tripping over both feet. I guess I only had a few minutes to wait until I was either believed and freed . . . or executed.

* * *

"McGregor, get in here!"

I looked up. Mr. McCully was standing at his office door. Calling me "McGregor" was bad, but his expression had softened a few more notches, right down to only really annoyed. I had learned to read his expressions. I guess practice makes perfect.

I scurried into his office. I almost sat down, but stopped myself in time — he never wanted kids to sit until he told them to.

"Sit," he said as he sank into his chair; I did the same. "I've talked to some of the students."

"And they told you I didn't do anything wrong?" I asked hopefully.

"Two of them did."

"That's great!" I beamed, feeling instant relief.

"But four of them didn't share that view."

"I-I don't understand," I stammered. "How many people did you talk to?"

"Six."

"What did the others say?"

"Two were just confused about what happened."

"I can understand that. It was confusing," I confirmed.

"And the last two said you were picking on the boy and it was all your fault."

"They're wrong! I wasn't picking on anybody!"

"They told me what they saw."

"They saw wrong! Let me talk to them!"

He laughed. "Fat chance. I'm not going to give you the opportunity to change anybody's mind."

"I wouldn't do that!" I protested. "Did you ask the other guy what happened?"

"I tried to speak to him at the time, and he didn't have much to say. Besides, what he says doesn't prove anything," Mr. McCully said.

"Maybe he'd tell you he started it and . . ." I stopped when I realized the chances of this were slim to none.

"So I'm left with a dilemma. I could still suspend you for fighting."

"But I wasn't —"

He raised his hands to silence me. "It doesn't matter whether he struck you first or not, you *were* rolling around on the ground with him."

"So you'd suspend him, too?" I questioned.

"Of course not . . . poor fellow has enough to deal with. Besides, this is his first brush with the office . . . unlike you."

"But you said in the meeting with my parents that I was starting fresh this year!" I argued. "That we'd all just forget about what happened last year."

He nodded slowly. "You are correct. I promised you a new beginning." He paused and looked at me hard. "And I'll keep my word."

"Then you're not going to suspend me?"

He shook his head and, despite my best efforts to suppress it, I burst into a smile.

"And if you're not going to suspend me, then you don't have to call my parents, right?"

"Again correct."

My smile got bigger and I rose to my feet, anxious to get out of there and head for second-period class.

"Sit down," he ordered. Instantly I plopped back down. "Just because I'm not going to suspend you, or call your parents, doesn't mean you're walking out of here without a consequence."

I wondered how many detentions I was going to get. I prayed they'd be over and done with before basketball tryouts started.

"And I don't think giving you detentions would be the thing to do," he continued.

"You don't?"

"Unless you want some?"

"No!" I practically screamed.

"Good, because I've thought of something else."

I didn't like his tone of voice or the smirk that spread across his face.

"What are you thinking of?" I asked nervously.

"Do you know the boy you were fighting with?" Mr. McCully asked.

"I don't know him, and I wasn't fighting, honest!"

"Regardless. His name is David Ross and he's new to our school. He's in grade eight, and the two of you are in the same homeroom, have three classes together, and share the same lunch period."

"Great," I muttered. I was hoping I'd never have to see him again.

"Yes, it is great, because it'll make it easier for you to be his host."

"His what?" I asked.

"His host. A student who acts as a guide to a

new student. Didn't we assign one to you last year?"

"No, I don't think so . . . wait a second . . . that's right, there was *Bradley*."

"That's right, and he has volunteered to be a host again this year. Didn't you find it helpful to have somebody show you around until you got used to the school?"

"A little, I guess," I said. A little is actually the amount of help Bradley gave me. He showed me to my classes my first day, told me where the washrooms were, and that was it. Of course, that was all I really wanted from him. The only people who liked Bradley were teachers.

"So?" Mr. McCully asked.

"You want me to be nice to some guy who punched me?" I asked in amazement. My plan had been to stay as far away from him as possible.

"His host . . . a guide."

"You're joking, right?"

A perplexed look came over Mr. McCully. "Am I known amongst the students as somebody with a wonderful sense of humor who just loves *joking* around?" Mr. McCully asked.

I tried to stifle a laugh, which escaped in a muffled snort. Other than his fashion sense which included wearing white sweat socks with everything, including brown dress shoes, there was nothing funny about Mr. McCully at all.

"That's what I thought. So you are assigned as

David's host. If you hurry now you can catch him on the way to second period. You two have math together."

I got to my feet and went to open the door, but paused at the door. What was I going to say to this guy?

"Do you have any questions?" Mr. McCully asked. "Because if you do I'm sure we could discuss it more. Perhaps we could even include your parents in the conversation?"

"That's okay," I said hastily. Without giving him a chance to say another word, I turned on my heels and left his office. I thought I could feel him smirk as I closed the door behind me.

Chapter 3

"Hey, wait up!" I yelled down the hall, and a dozen kids, including David, looked in my direction. He turned back around and kept going.

"Wait up . . . David!" I called out.

He instantly spun the chair around, almost bumping into a couple of little seveners who jumped off to the side. I hurried to catch up.

"You want to go again?" he snarled, holding his fists up.

I stopped in front of him, still far enough away to be out of punching range.

"No, I . . . I˙. . . just . . ." I looked at the little cluster of kids who had also stopped. They were watching us, maybe waiting for round two to begin. "Beat it or none of you will live to see second period!" I threatened.

They practically jumped out of their shoes and scurried down the corridor.

"Big man, threatening little seveners," he said. "You're pretty tough . . . to look at."

I felt my temper rising and clenched my hands and . . . I swallowed hard and took a deep breath. I wasn't going to get into this. Not here, not now, and not with him.

"Even without the use of legs I can still kick your butt down the hall."

"I didn't come here to fight."

"Well, you're wasting your time if you've come to apologize."

"Apologize!" I repeated in shock. "You're the one who punched me!"

"Yeah, and I'll do it again if you don't go away!" he threatened as he moved slightly toward me.

I backed up half a step. "Can you just cool it for a second?"

He gave me a hard look. "What do you want?"

"I'm your host," I muttered under my breath.

"My *what*?"

"Your host. I'm supposed to show you around the school, answer your questions, and stuff."

"I don't need anybody, especially you, to take care of me! I don't need any special treatment."

"It's not special. All new students get a host," I explained.

His jaw relaxed a little and the glare in his eyes faded slightly. "*All* new students?"

I nodded. "I had one last year. It's hard to find your way around this school. It was designed by an idiot. Even the numbers don't make sense. It took me months to find my way around."

"So you're saying that either it really is badly laid out . . . or you're not too quick." He spun his chair around again and started off down the hall.

This was insane. Did I need extra grief? I started to walk away myself when I thought about having to go home to face my parents if McCully found out I'd blown off his offer and decided to phone home. I hurried after David and fell in a step behind him.

"You're going the wrong way," I said.

"How do you even know where I'm going?"

"We have the same second period."

"How do you know that?" he demanded.

"McCully told me — we actually have three classes together and lunch."

"Great," he muttered, and I couldn't help but smile at the way he'd reacted — exactly like I had at the news. "Who's McCully? Is he the one who stopped the fight?"

"That's him. He's the vice-principal."

"And why would you volunteer for this job?"

"Yeah, right, give me a break," I snickered.

"Then what?" he questioned.

"McCully volunteered me."

"So is this like punishment, you having to be my guide dog?"

"It sure beats a suspension," I said.

"He was threatening to suspend you?"

I nodded. "I thought I was gone."

David started to laugh again, a hearty, deep sound that echoed off the lockers and down the hall. "So let me get this straight. I punch you half a dozen times, and all I get is an 'are you all right, son?' but he threatens to suspend *you* for being punched?"

"Yeah, that pretty well sums it up," I admitted.

"Welcome to Wheelchair World."

"I don't understand."

"I didn't think you would."

The bell rang to mark the beginning of second period and I jumped.

"Are you always so nervous?" he asked.

"I am about being late." I was now going to have to face McCully for the second time in two periods. "Just what I need, another trip to the office for a late slip."

"Don't sweat it. We'll just tell the teacher you were showing me to class," David said.

"That won't help. Late is late no matter what the reason."

"We'll see. Which way do we go?"

"It's back through those doors," I said, pointing back the way we came.

David spun away, and I had to walk quickly to catch up with him. The halls were almost empty now.

Suddenly David skidded to a stop and I almost bumped into him. I didn't want to do that again.

"Steps," he said.

"I'm sorry . . . I just didn't think about it."

"No problem. There's only three of them. Three I can do." He spun around and quickly wheeled away up the corridor. Again the chair turned and he started back, pumping his hands on the wheels to gain speed. I watched in wide-eyed amazement as he rocketed toward the steps. He shot off the edge and flew out, landing with a thunderous crash on the floor at the bottom. Teetering precariously, he almost turned over, but managed to stay on his wheels.

One of the classroom doors popped open. A teacher poked her head out, gave me a nasty look, and retreated back into her room.

"Are you coming?" David called out.

I jumped down the three steps and caught him just as he was going past the hall where we had to turn. Instinctively, I grabbed the back of the chair and pointed him in the right direction.

Suddenly the chair stopped and I practically toppled over it.

"Don't you ever do that again!" David yelled.

"I was just trying to —"

"I don't care what you were trying to do! You don't ever push me! This isn't some stroller! You got it?" he demanded.

I backed away a couple of steps to get out of the

range of his fists. I could still feel the place in my stomach where he'd punched me this morning.

"I got it . . . and it won't happen again."

"It better not. Now let's get to class."

The class was just down the hall, and I motioned for David to stop by the door. I opened it slowly and quietly. The teacher stopped mid-sentence as I walked in. Everybody was staring at me.

"Sorry I'm late," I said.

Mrs. Burk glared at me. I'd had her for math in grade seven, and she and I knew each other a lot better than either of us wanted.

"Do you have a late slip?" she asked gruffly.

I shook my head.

"Go and get one . . . *now*."

"Do I need one, too?" David asked as I stepped aside and he came in behind me.

Mrs. Burk's expression quickly changed from angry to surprised to confused.

"Really, it's all my fault we're late. I got all turned around and my new friend . . . um . . . um . . . "

"Sean," I chipped in.

"Yeah, Sean here helped me find my way. I'd still be wandering the halls if it wasn't for him." David's voice was soft and buttery. "He was only late because of me."

Mrs. Burk rushed over to David. "Here, let me help," she offered and took hold of the back of his chair. She shouldn't have done that . . . I braced myself for an explosion . . . but nothing. Instead, he smiled sweetly at her. Mrs. Burk wheeled him to an empty desk in the first row.

She returned to the front of the class while I remained standing by the door.

"Are you going to join us?" she asked me.

"You mean I don't need a —"

"Sit down."

I didn't wait for any more instructions. There was an empty seat right beside David, and I settled in alongside him. This was the first time I'd ever sat in the front row voluntarily — usually I was only there if a teacher wanted to keep an eye on me. When Mrs. Burk looked away, David gave me a nod and a knowing smile, an expression like "I told you."

Mrs. Burk started back into her lesson. She wasn't talking about math, but how she ran her class. This was just a rerun of what she lectured us about last year — absolutely no marks or writing in the textbook, proper covers, everything in pencil, erasing marks had to be complete, blab, blab, blab. She was a real neat freak. I almost thought she'd prefer a neat mistake to a messy correct answer.

I cast a sideways glance at David. He had his books open and was taking notes! What sort of a goof would take notes about junk like this?

Just then he saw me looking at him and turned

his notebook so I could see what he was working on. It wasn't notes, but a half-finished drawing . . . of Mrs. Burk! It was a fantastic likeness, although the hair was frizzier and the glasses bigger, sort of like a cartoon version of her. He turned his notebook back around and continued to work.

My eyes fell on his chair, and for a split second I was thrown. It was like I'd forgotten he was in a wheelchair. I looked down at his legs and then I saw his shoes — they were exactly the same as mine! Very expensive, high-top Nike basketball shoes. They looked brand new, not a scuff on them. But then, he didn't exactly wear them out, now, did he? But why spend so much money on something that would never be used? I looked down at my shoes and then over at his. They even looked to be about the same size, eleven. He had big feet.

Next I cast a sideways glance at his legs. They were very long. I pulled my legs back under the desk, the way his were, to compare them. I couldn't tell for sure but it looked like his were longer. Was he taller than me?

He looked very athletic — like he'd been pumping iron or something. Maybe the iron wheels of his chair. I put a hand on my sore stomach. No wonder he'd knocked the wind out of me.

Just then the bell rang, signaling the end of the period. Chairs scraped and books closed and people took to their feet.

"Hold on!" Mrs. Burk called out and the noise

subsided. "I want you to know that I won't be giving any surprise tests this year."

A cheer went up from the class. She raised her hand to silence everybody.

"So be prepared for an *announced* test at the end of the week." The resulting groans were even bigger than the preceding cheers. "Class dismissed!"

Kids grumbled as they left the room to head to their period three classes.

"Where to now?" David asked.

"I think we have science together. Let me look at your schedule just to be sure."

He unfolded it and handed it to me.

"*Is* there . . . *anything* . . . I can help you . . . *with*?" Mrs. Burk asked as she came over to us.

Why was she talking that way?

"We're okay," David replied.

"Good!" she said loudly. "I'm *available* . . . to *help* . . . *any time*."

"*Fine* . . . thank you!" David said, repeating her volume and phrasing.

"We better get going," I added. "We both have science next and it's on the far side of the school. I don't want to be late again."

David put his books into a pack attached to the back of his chair. I picked up my books, and we started for the door as a class of seveners started to head in. They jumped out of the way as David rolled through them. I wondered how many of them had seen the brawl this morning and didn't want to be part of round two.

"Good luck!" Mrs. Burk called out. I turned around to see her waving to us, a big smile across her face. I gave a little wave back. David continued rolling along and I hurried after him.

"What did she mean, 'good luck?' I think I can find science."

"That wasn't aimed at you," David said.

"What do you mean?"

"Forget it, you wouldn't understand," he replied as he continued to roll along.

I was getting tired of this "I wouldn't understand" crap. We moved along in uneasy silence, the noise of his wheels softly whizzing the only sound. I just had to show him to a few more classes — today, and maybe tomorrow — and this would all be over.

"Here we are," I said, stopping at the door to the science room. The bell rang loudly. "And not a second too soon."

Chapter 4

"So how come you aren't wearing your fancy shoes today?" Scott asked as we stood together outside the school.

"They're in my backpack," I said, motioning to my pack. "I wore them special for yesterday, you know, first day. From now on, I'll only wear them for gym, basketball, and games."

"When do the tryouts begin?" Scott asked.

"Next week, I think."

"And you want to make the team."

"Of course, I want to make the team!" I exclaimed.

"More than anything."

"Yes," I answered, nodding my head emphatically.

"Come on," Scott said as he started to walk. I

trailed behind as he walked through the gate and off school property. "Then you can't afford to get in trouble."

"That's for sure."

"And I'm going to help you stay out of trouble," Scott said.

"You?" I asked in amazement.

"I just did."

"How did you . . . ?" I stopped as Scott pulled out a package of cigarettes and put one in his mouth.

"If I was caught smoking on school property and you were standing with me, then you'd get in trouble, too," he said. He took out some matches and lit the cigarette.

"Wouldn't it just be easier if you didn't smoke when you were with me?" I asked.

"Don't lecture me. No one's forcing you to smoke, unless you want . . .?" He offered me the package.

I coughed. "I'm getting more than I want just standing here beside you. Can't you get down-wind?"

Scott smirked, took a deep drag from his ciga-rette, and blew a puff of smoke in my direction. I reached out to smack him and he knocked my hand away, dancing out of my reach.

"What are you aiming for, a fight every day?" Scott joked.

"I'm aiming for no fights, any day."

"Then you're off to a bad start. Me today and that wheelchair kid yesterday."

"This wasn't exactly a fight."

"Neither was the one yesterday. For it to be a fight, you would have had to get in at least one shot at him."

"Shut up!" I snapped angrily.

"Sorry," he apologized and I knew he meant it.

Scott was always saying and doing stupid things, but he usually felt rotten afterward. He really wasn't a bad guy. He just had bad judgment. Then again, who was I to talk?

"You never did tell me, how many detentions did you get for that little scrap?" Scott asked.

"None."

"None? So how *did* old man McCully punish you?"

"I was assigned to be a host."

"What's a host?" Scott asked.

"You know, somebody who helps a new student find their way around."

"You a host?" he laughed. "So who are you hosting?"

I took a deep breath. "The kid in the wheelchair," I said quietly.

"Come on, seriously, who?"

"I told you."

Scott shook his head and smiled. "That McCully is really warped. So what do you have to do, like show him to classes and be his friend?"

"Nobody said anything about being his friend. I'll show him around for a few days and that'll be it."

"I guess that's better than detentions."

"Or a suspension."

"McCully was threatening to suspend you?"

"Getting ready to call my parents."

"Then I guess you did get off easy . . . this time," Scott said.

"This time?" I asked.

"Sure. The next time you get in trouble —"

"There isn't going to be any next time!" I jumped in.

Scott laughed. He obviously didn't believe it. Then again, it did seem like a long shot.

"So, no skipping classes?" Scott questioned.

"None."

"All your homework is going to be completed?"

"Yes."

"You're not going to talk back to teachers, or be late, or get into fights?"

I paused before answering. Scott had just about listed everything I'd done wrong last year.

"You think you can avoid fights?" he pressed on.

"I'm going to try hard . . . at least until after basketball season is over."

"How long is that?"

"The season goes until December."

"That's about three months." He shrugged. "Maybe you can last that long . . . but I wouldn't bet any money on it."

I looked down at my watch. There was only a few minutes until the bell would ring, and I had to go and find David.

"I better get going," I said.

Scott dropped his cigarette butt to the ground and stubbed it out with the tip of his shoe. "Going to play host?"

"That's the idea. Are you coming?"

He pulled another cigarette out of the pack. "Not yet. It's not me who has to stay out of trouble. Have a *good* day."

Chapter 5

The ball left my fingers in a perfect arch, rotating ever so slightly as it flew, and then "swish," nothing but net.

"Nice shot."

I turned and was surprised to see David sitting on the sidewalk at the end of my driveway.

"Thanks," I said as I retrieved the ball. What was he doing here? How did he know where I live?

"Here." David held up his hands for a pass. Gently I lobbed the ball to him. He examined the ball, turning it in his hands, and then bounced it twice. "Expensive ball."

"It was a birthday present."

He nodded. He launched a shot, and it hit the rim and went off to the side.

"Good try," I offered as I corralled the rebound.

"Even I don't get them all in."

"Big news! Even Michael Jordan doesn't make 'em all. Toss me the ball . . . and this time don't throw it like a wimp."

I'd show him a pass! I shot a chest pass, straight and hard and as flat as a frozen rope. It made a crisp sound as he caught it. Part of me was glad it didn't take his head right off. Part of me was disappointed it didn't. David spun the ball in his hands, cast an eye on the net, and then shot — high, arching, spinning, nothing but net! Lucky shot. I grabbed the ball.

"Let's see it again," David said.

I hesitated and then tossed it to him again, not quite as hard as the last time.

He bounced it twice and then put up another shot, again, nothing but net.

"Not bad," I admitted.

"Are these lines in the right places?" He was referring to the markings painted on my driveway to show the key and three-point line.

"Exactly right."

"And your father let you do it?" he asked.

"Let me? He insisted on it. My father loves basketball. He played for his college team. I think it was his dream to be a pro basketball player instead of an insurance salesman."

"And you like playing, too?" David said.

"I'm trying out for the school team. That's why I'm practicing."

"You're a forward."

"Yeah, how did you know?" I asked in surprise.

"You're not tall enough for center and too tall to be a guard. Besides, I was watching as I was coming up, and you seem to be working the side of the key the most. Have you thought of going with a low post fade-away hook shot?"

"A low post fade-away hook shot?" I repeated the words, not really understanding what he meant.

"Here, give me the ball," he said. I tossed it to him and he wheeled over to the side of the key. He stopped at just about the spot where I was taking a lot of my shots. He turned the chair so his back was to the net and threw up a hook shot. It bounced off the backboard and into the net. Either he was really, really lucky . . . or good.

"Like that," he said.

He moved out of the way, and I settled into the spot where he had shot. Awkwardly I threw it up and it clanged hard against the board and shot away.

"Good try. Even *I* don't get them *all* in," he said with a smirk and laughed. I almost laughed myself but realized that laugh was aimed at me.

Over the past three days, as I helped David get to classes, I'd gotten to know him a bit. One of the things I'd learned was that he could make conversation and joke around one second and then take a shot at me or somebody else — well, at least a verbal shot — the next second.

Actually, I guess I really wasn't helping him as much as sort of walking along beside him. He knew his way around after the first day. Other than showing him his classes, I couldn't figure out what else this whole hosting thing was about, so I left him on his own. He didn't seem to need a baby-sitter.

"If you can get that fade-away hook to drop consistently, it works in combination with your jump shot or a move to the hoop. They may have to double down on you, or at least get outside help, and that lets you rotate it back to the outside for a shot while you crash the boards for the rebound."

I gave him a questioning look. "You know a lot about basketball."

"Yeah. Why shouldn't I?"

"Well . . ." Had I said something wrong again?

He shook his head slowly. "I'm . . . in . . . a . . . wheelchair . . . I'm . . . not . . . stupid . . . or . . . dumb," he paused on each word. It reminded me of the way Mrs. Burk had spoken to him. Actually, a couple of the teachers talked to him that way, sort of slow, like he wouldn't understand if they spoke normally.

I was suddenly embarrassed at what I'd said and could feel myself flushing. "I just meant . . . you know, it sounds like you know a lot . . . more than most people."

"More than almost *all* people," he said. "Here, give me the ball again." I tossed it to him. He wheeled farther out, still off to the same side, and laid up another hook shot. Again, it hit the backboard and dropped through the hoop.

"That hook shot will work well all the way from tight inside to all the way out here, but it's best to pick two spots, one right at the side where I took the first one and a second farther out. Mark the spots so you can get your arm used to those two distances, you know, get the rhythm of the shots so they become automatic. You can't be thinking about it when somebody's in your face."

"I'm pretty good in traffic," I said.

"You've got good size, but practicing by yourself isn't nearly as good as working against somebody. Do you play much or just practice on your own?"

"Mostly on my own," I admitted.

"You need the game action. Aren't there courts around here aside from the one painted on your driveway?"

"There's a court down by the school," I said reluctantly. I didn't like to go there that much. Last year the guys who were on a school team, including a couple of the jerks I'd had fights with, hung out there.

"Maybe you need to go down there and play some pickup," David suggested.

"It's hard to get a game. There's always older kids who claim the nets."

"If they let you play, that's even better. Best

way to improve is to play over your head. And even if they're bigger than you, it's almost impossible to block that hook shot I showed you. Here, give me the ball again."

I tossed him the ball.

"Now get between me and the basket like you're going to try to stuff me."

"Sure." I ambled over to his side.

David looked at me. "Is that the way you try to block somebody? Don't you usually put your arms up, or were you hoping to stop it with your face?"

Reluctantly I put up my arms. This felt stupid. I towered over his wheelchair and there was no way in the world he was going to put a shot over me. His arm went up at the same instant he wheeled slightly away from me, and the ball arched high over my outstretched fingertips, hit the backboard, and whooshed through the mesh. My mouth dropped open.

"I think you can put your arms down now," David said. "But that's got to be your biggest problem."

"What's my biggest problem?"

"You don't react quickly enough."

"What do you mean?" I demanded.

"You just stood there and watched my shot. You didn't go for the rebound."

"There wasn't a rebound."

"But if there was one you'd never have gotten it. The same as when you shoot. You freeze after your shot."

"I don't freeze!"

"Sure you do. I watched you shoot a dozen shots before you saw me."

"Maybe I was just concentrating on my shot," I snapped back.

"Concentration is one thing, but once the ball is in flight there's no point in standing there like you're posing for a camera. Instead of standing there like it's some sort of Kodak moment, you have to get moving — follow your shot, go for the rebound." He paused. "Unless you never miss."

"Of course, I . . ." I let the sentence trail off as I realized he was taking another shot at me.

"Most of the game isn't about what shots you make but what happens after a miss. Following up, chasing loose balls, rebounding, making the broken plays into points. Doesn't that make sense?"

"I guess so," I reluctantly admitted.

David looked at his watch. "But I don't have any more time to be a coach."

Good, I thought, because nobody's asking you to be.

"I was headed to the store. Wanna come?" David asked.

I was just getting ready to stop taking shots — my mom had been bugging me to go in and do my piano practice . . . maybe she'd let me go to the store. I'd really worked up a sweat, and a Coke would go down good. Besides, it would sure beat the heck out of practicing the piano.

"Well, do you want to come?" he asked again.

"Let me check," I said.

I ran up the driveway, bounded up the stairs, crossed the porch, and went through the front door.

"Mom! I'm going to go to the store!" I yelled. "I'll do my piano when I get back!"

"Hold on, young man!" she called back as she came out of the kitchen. "You promised that you'd start right after school."

"But a friend dropped by," I said.

"Friend?" she asked. I knew that tone of voice. She wondered if it was Scott, or maybe Gavin or Nick. People she didn't want me to go anywhere with.

"It's David."

"David?"

"You know, that kid I mentioned. The one I'm hosting."

"The boy in the wheelchair?"

I nodded my head. Over supper one night I'd told them I had "volunteered" for the job without telling them why. They seemed pleased.

"Well . . . I guess it would be okay. He probably doesn't have that many friends."

"Thanks. I'll be back soon."

I ran out the door before she had a chance to change her mind. With any luck, today's piano practice would just sort of go away.

"Let's go," I said.

"Your ball," David said as he tossed it to me.

"Yeah, thanks. I better put it away."

"Don't put it away. Dribble it. When I was working on my crossover, I used to practically sleep with my ball."

Crossover? Obviously he couldn't do a crossover while he was in his chair. That meant at one time he could walk. I wondered what had happened, but . . . nope, I wasn't going to ask him.

We started off down the street. The ball made a ping each time it hit the pavement. This ping was punctuated by a rhythmic clicking as his chair rolled over the cracks between the sidewalk squares.

"Do you live far from here?" I asked.

"No, just a few streets over. Chambers, 170 Chambers Avenue."

"Did your family just move in?"

"We moved in a week before school started. Do you know if the variety store over on Silverthorn has steps?" David asked.

"I never really noticed."

"You probably wouldn't, but it's something I always have to keep in mind."

"There's another store just a block that way," I said, pointing the other way from where we were headed. "It's closer."

"I know that store. It has three steps up. I can

go down them okay, as you probably remember from the hall." He paused. "But I can't get up them very easily."

"I guess we'll find out soon enough about the other store," I said.

"Your family hasn't been here very long either, right?"

"Not long, just under a year . . . how did you know?"

"You told me."

"I did?"

"Yeah. You said you had a host last year, so I knew it couldn't be that long."

I nodded my head. That explained one mystery, but I still didn't know how he knew where I lived.

"Did I mention that I lived on Rosethorn?" I asked.

"No."

"Then how did you know where I lived?"

"I didn't. I was just going to the store and saw you on the driveway."

The store was just up ahead. I held my head a little higher to try to see if there were steps. I couldn't tell for sure, but I didn't think so.

"No stairs that I can see," David said, confirming my thoughts.

He rolled up to the door and stopped. He moved over to the side slightly and awkwardly pulled the door open.

"You want to give me a hand here?" he asked.

"Oh, sure," I said, jumping over to pull the door open. "I just thought that, you know, that you wouldn't want me to." I was thinking about how he reacted when I tried to push his chair.

"Why not? Don't you hold the door open for other people sometimes?"

"Yeah, of course."

"I'm no different. Maybe on the way out I'll hold it open for *you*."

David went into the store and I followed behind. I hadn't realized how hot it really was outside until I was hit by a wave of cool air from the air conditioner. David stopped at the cooler and slid open the door.

"What do you want?' he asked.

"A Coke."

"Good choice." He pulled out two cans. "My treat."

"That's okay, I have money."

"I want to pay. Okay?"

"Sure."

"You can pay the next time."

Who said there would be a next time?

David paid the guy behind the counter, gathered up his change, and went out through the door. He held it open for me.

"The pushing side of the door is always easier for me," he said. "Is there someplace shady where we can sit and drink these? It's hard for me to drink and wheel at the same time . . . I end up going in circles," he said with a chuckle.

"Sure, there's a nice spot under some trees behind the school."

"Sounds good." David bounced off the curb and onto the street. A car blew its horn and swerved. David made a gesture with his hand to indicate he wasn't any happier with the driver. He continued across the road and another car drastically slowed down to let him pass. He popped the front wheels of the chair into the air and bumped up onto the sidewalk on the other side. I still stood on the curb. I'd seen the cars coming and waited. I was still waiting for another car to pass. It went by, and, after looking both ways, I proceeded across the street.

"That was close," I said as I caught up to him.

"What was close?"

"That car. It didn't miss you by much."

"Nah, he missed me by a mile. I saw him all the way."

I hadn't noticed David look in any direction before crossing.

We went around the side of the school and passed right by the basketball court. It was deserted.

"I thought you said it was always crowded," David questioned.

"Usually it is. I guess it's too hot for people to play."

"How about if we work up more of a thirst?"

David asked.

"What do you mean?"

"Let's shoot some hoops before we have our Cokes."

"Some hoops?"

"Yeah. How about a game of twenty-one?"

"Me against you?"

"You see anybody else around here?" David asked. I could tell by his tone that he was getting impatient.

"That would be okay," I agreed.

I liked playing on this court. The backboards were solid and the pavement more even than my driveway, which was cracking in a few places. I would like to have played here more last year. I wondered if it was deserted now, not so much because of the heat, but because those jokers played at the high school now.

I opened up the gate surrounding the court and we went inside. I held it open so David could follow in after me.

"You take first ball," David suggested. "Think of it as *your* handicap."

I walked to take the foul line and spun the ball in my hands, getting ready to shoot. I thought about his temper and wondered how he'd take losing. Maybe I should keep it close, just beat him by a little bit.

"Hold on a second," David said. "How about if we make this game a little more interesting?"

"What did you have in mind?"

"A little wager." He smiled.

"Go on."

"Loser pays for lunch tomorrow." He paused. "We are going to eat lunch together, aren't we?"

I nodded. "We could . . . I never turn down a lunch that somebody else is paying for."

"You must have misunderstood me," David said. "The arrangement is that the *loser* is going to pay."

Even if he couldn't play, at least he knew how to trash talk. I put up my shot and it dropped for the first point of the game.

Chapter 6

"How about we sit over there?" David suggested, pointing at the far end of the cafeteria.

"Where?"

"I see a table that looks interesting. Follow me."

He threaded his way through the tables and chairs filled with kids eating their lunches. A couple of times he had to ask people to pull in their chairs to let him get by. He stopped in front of a table where three girls were sitting. I didn't recognize them — they looked like they were in grade seven. There were still three empty seats at the table.

"Hi, girls. Do you believe in love at first sight . . . or do you want me to roll by again?" David asked.

I practically fell over backward.

"What did you say?" one of the girls asked.

"I said, do you believe in —"

"He's wondering if anybody's using these empty seats." I practically yelled, cutting him off before he could repeat it again.

David turned to me and chuckled. "Yeah, are these seats taken? Not that I need one myself."

One of the girls blushed noticeably, and the other two looked a bit thrown by what he'd said.

"I guess you can have them," one of the girls answered nervously.

David pushed one seat slightly over to the side so his chair could slide under the table. I put my things down on the table in front of the seat beside him. That way there was a free seat between me and the three girls.

"I'll be back in a minute," I said.

"No rush, it'll just give me more time to get to know our three new friends."

New friends? I moved back across the crowded cafeteria. I couldn't help notice how much easier it was to move between the kids and tables and chairs now that I wasn't trailing David. I joined the line to buy lunch — for myself and David.

It had been a close game, but I'd lost by three points. The problem wasn't that I played badly, because I hadn't, but that David shot so well. Naturally, he couldn't pounce on the rebounds as well, as he had to shoot from farther out, but he was just a natural shooter. And once he got to the free-throw line, he kept popping them. And I had thought that I was going to take it easy on him.

Right after he potted the winning shot, he offered to call off the bet; he said he didn't like taking money from a friend. Him calling me a friend shocked me more than losing. But I guess being new in the neighborhood and school, he really didn't know anybody else. I remembered how good it was to finally start hanging out with Scott — not that I was planning on hanging out with David. I didn't necessarily like it, but I was going to honor our bet. After all, a bet's a bet. Besides, like I told him, if we played again, I was counting on him to pay off when he lost.

Later on, when I was thinking about it, I was pretty happy there hadn't been anybody around to see the game. I knew he beat me because he could shoot, but anybody who didn't know the game might have thought it was because I stunk. Imagine losing to a guy in a wheelchair! I was sure there was still enough talk around the school about our fight, not that I'd heard any of it myself.

I grabbed a tray and slid it along the rails until I came to the front of the line.

"Could I have two orders of fries, a hot dog, and a burger?"

"You're either very hungry or you're buying for your girlfriend, too," the lady behind the counter said.

"For a friend."

I put everything on the tray and then added two Cokes. I didn't know if these Cokes counted as part of the bet or for the one he bought me before the game.

"Mr. McGregor, how are things going?" I recognized the voice and turned to see Mr. McCully. He was wearing a wonderful little number that included a plaid shirt and striped tie.

"Good, really good. I haven't been sent to the office again."

"That would be an accomplishment if this was more than lunch on the fourth day. That *is* quite a lunch you have there."

"It's not just for me. I'm getting David his lunch as well. You know it's a lot harder for him with the line and carrying the tray and everything," I said. I didn't want him, or anybody else, to know the real reason I was doing this.

Mr. McCully nodded and opened his mouth to say something, but I could see David talking and laughing with those girls, and I wanted to get back before he said anything really dumb. "I've gotta get going," I said quickly. "Don't want the food to get cold."

I could feel McCully's eyes on my back as I made my way to the table. The three girls were laughing when I got there. Whatever David had said was certainly amusing them. I always felt stupid around girls, and I never knew what to talk to them about. I put down the tray, and, as I started to divide the food up, I saw that he had his drawing pad out again. He was drawing a picture of one of the girls, and the other two were peering over his shoulder.

"Sean, I want to introduce you to our three new friends. This is Christina, Caroline, and Lisa," David said as he pointed to each one while he continued to sketch. I mumbled hello and they mumbled back, paying much more attention to the drawing than to me.

"I was just offering our services to help them get to know their way around the school or if they had any questions about how things run around here," David said.

"You were?"

"Sure. I was wondering, are you three going to the start-of-the-year dance tomorrow night?"

The three of them looked at each other and giggled. "Maybe . . . I guess," one of them, I couldn't remember which was which, twittered.

"Well, you should," David said enthusiastically. "And maybe you can all save a dance for me. I can totally guarantee that I won't step on your feet. As well, you should know I'm the only kid in the whole school who has his own set of wheels."

They all giggled nervously as David continued his sketch. His work was really starting to take shape, and an unmistakable image of the one girl was quickly forming on his page. He was like one of those people who sit on lawn chairs at tourist places and offer to draw your picture for twenty-five dollars. He was good enough that he could do that . . . and he wouldn't even need the lawn chair to sit on.

"Oh, and I guess I should mention to you, Sean, you won the bet."

"I did?" I had no idea what he was talking about.

"You know, when you bet me that we could fool people into thinking we were really having a fight and I didn't think we could. Well, I was wrong, these girls really believed we were fighting."

"You were there?" I asked.

"Everybody was. And it wasn't just us you fooled. Everybody thought it was for real," another one of the girls chirped.

"So did the vice-principal," David added. "We almost got in trouble because he doesn't like people to even play fight."

"You're both really good actors, especially you," one of the girls said, pointing at me.

"Me?"

"Yeah, we really thought David was hurting you. You groaned so realistically when he pretended to punch you. It was like you were really hurt."

"Hey, what about me?" David demanded.

"You were good, too," another offered and the other two nodded in agreement.

"Thank you," David said. "But I still think I'm

a much better artist than I am an actor. Here," he said as he passed the picture over to the girl he was drawing.

"Isn't it wonderful!" she beamed.

"Can you do me next?" one of the other two asked.

I lost interest in the conversation as I caught sight of Scott moving across the cafeteria. This wasn't his lunch period so what was he doing here? He saw me, too, gave a big wave, and changed course to come in my direction. I could only imagine what he was going to say about me sitting with David and three seveners.

"Sean, my man, what's shaking?" he yelled from three tables away. Heads turned to watch him walk by. Scott loved making an entrance. He grabbed the seat David had pushed out of the way, spun it around, and straddled it so he was sitting right beside me.

"What are you doing here?" I asked.

"Taking a bit of an early lunch. Wanted to talk to you. Aren't you returning phone calls these days?"

"You called?"

"Three or four times."

"I guess my parents forgot to tell me," I said. Actually I had got one message that he'd called, but not that many. But it didn't surprise me that I wasn't told about the other times.

"I haven't even seen much of you since the fight."

All three girls burst out laughing. Scott looked at them like they were from another planet. Now that he was in grade eight, Scott had decided seveners were some sort of lower life form.

"What's so funny?" he asked them.

"It wasn't a *real* fight. They were just fooling around."

"They were what?" Scott asked.

"It was a play fight," David said as he wheeled out from under the table and turned so he was facing Scott.

"It's . . . it's . . . you," he muttered. I don't think Scott had recognized David before because his wheelchair had been tucked under the table.

"Of course, it's me. Who else would I be?"

Scott turned to me "The fight wasn't real?"

"It wasn't a fight," I said. Like Scott had pointed out the other day, I would have had to have taken at least one swing for it to be called a fight.

"But . . . but . . ." he sputtered.

"You told me yourself it wasn't a fight," I said. "Right?"

Scott shook his head in dismay. "Whatever. It doesn't matter to me. So what are you doing *here*?"

"This is my lunch period." Of course, that wasn't what he meant — he was talking about being with David and the three seveners.

"So I guess you're being a good little host."

I didn't know what to answer. I was afraid

David was going to mention my lost bet.

"Shouldn't you get going?" I asked Scott, trying to get rid of him.

"Yeah, I guess so. I was just cutting through when I saw you. I'm meeting Nick. We're going out to grab a bite and a game of pool. You want to come?"

"Not enough time."

"There is if you skip your next class or . . . oh, I forgot, you're not doing things like that this year," he said with a smirk on his face. "See you later."

We watched Scott pick his way across the cafeteria. He didn't move around anybody. He just expected them to get out of his way. Is that how I looked last year?

He was almost at the exit doors when Mr. McCully popped his head back in. Scott ducked behind a bunch of kids so he couldn't be seen. Suddenly he didn't look so cool. Moving from hiding spot to hiding spot, he made it out of the doors on the far side without being noticed.

"So he's a friend of yours?" David asked.

"Yeah, we hung out . . . last year."

"And is he always that way?"

"What way?"

"Stupid."

"Not always," I said. Most of the time, I thought to myself.

Chapter 7

I could feel the thumping pulse of the music as it rolled down the hall and entered into my body, lodging in my stomach. That wasn't good. My stomach was already upset, and the music seemed to cause my dinner to dance around even more. I still had no idea how I'd let David talk me into coming here. If nothing else, David was certainly persuasive.

"How late does the dance go?" David asked.

"Um . . . I think around nine."

"Come on, it's got to go later than that! A dance can't go for just two hours! Are you sure?"

"Not really," I admitted. Actually, I had no idea.

"How late did the dances go last year?"

"I can't remember," I answered. That wasn't a completely dishonest reply. I couldn't remember because I never knew. I had never been to a dance at Homelands. In fact, I'd never been to any dance anywhere. Sure, I'd taken a couple of trips around the dance floor with an aunt, or my mother, at a wedding, but that was it.

As we turned the corner of the hall we saw a line of kids standing at the gymnasium door, waiting to pay to go in. Mr. McCully was at the door, arms crossed, checking out everything and everybody. That was one reason for not coming that I hadn't mentioned to David — cutting down the number of meetings with McCully that I absolutely needed to have. We joined the back of the line and shuffled forward. David made small talk and joked around, and I just grunted in reply. I was too nervous to add anything. Funny, it was the same sort of nervous I got before a basketball game.

"Sean, this is a surprise! I didn't think you did the dance thing," Mr. McCully announced, catching me by surprise.

Sean! I don't remember him ever calling me by my first name. I tried to think of what to say, but no words came to mind.

Mr. McCully turned to David. "And how are you finding things here at Homelands?"

"Good, real good. Sean's really helped me settle in and get to know my way around."

Mr. McCully looked at me in a way I'd never seen before. He looked almost happy. I guess that was better than the usual look, but far more confusing. At least mad I understood.

"Well, it's a great night for a dance," he said as he took our tickets, ripped them in two and handed us back the torn stubs. "Sean, could I talk to you for a minute?"

"Sure," I answered hesitantly. I felt the palms of my hands start to sweat. Whatever he wanted couldn't be good, but I couldn't think of anything I'd done that could get me in trouble. I'd really been trying.

"I'll meet you inside," I said to David as he rolled in through the door.

Mr. McCully motioned for another teacher to take his place, and then I followed him as he walked over to the side, away from the crush of kids at the door.

"I haven't done anything wrong . . . really!" I protested.

He chuckled. "Sounds like you have a guilty conscience."

"I don't have a guilty anything."

"I believe you. I just wanted a moment alone to thank you," Mr. McCully said.

"Thank me? For what?" I asked, although I was so relieved I wasn't in trouble that I didn't really care what he was thanking me for.

"For helping David. I expected you to have a better year — keeping up your end of the bargain about staying out of trouble — but what you've been doing to help David has really impressed me."

Maybe coming to this dance wasn't such a stupid idea after all.

"Keep up the good work," Mr. McCully said.

"I'm going to try!"

"That's good to hear. Now go on in and enjoy yourself."

I hurried off into the gym. As I opened the door, the music flowed over me like a wave, pushed along by the pulsing lights that repeatedly split the darkness. I stepped inside. All along the walls were streamers and balloons. Up on the stage was a DJ wearing earphones. Just his head could be seen over the bank of speakers surrounding him. On the floor just beneath him was a table holding a few punch bowls and stacks of plastic cups. My mouth felt bone dry. As soon as I found David I wanted to go get something to drink.

I walked right across the gym, following the center line and moving around little clusters of kids. I knew almost all of them, but I was surprised to see how different they looked. Everybody was in dressier clothes. Almost all of the girls had their hair fancy, and even in the darkness I could see most were wearing makeup. They looked older . . . and taller. I realized they were all wearing big, clunky heels that made them tower even more over most of the boys. I nodded to a few people and said a couple of words as I craned my neck and scanned the room, trying to find David. It was hard to find anybody, but, with him being in a chair, he was closer to the ground and even harder to see.

As I ducked around another knot of people I was suddenly struck by the fact that despite the pounding music, there was almost nobody actually dancing. It definitely looked more like a "stand" than a "dance." The only exception was a small group of girls off to one side who were dancing with each other.

Out of the corner of my eye I saw David waving to me — and he was standing with Scott. I didn't know exactly why, but that made me nervous. This was another complication I didn't need.

"How's it going!" I yelled to Scott.

"What?" he hollered back.

I leaned forward so my mouth was practically against his ear. "Hello!"

He nodded. "Yeah, hello."

Just as I was about to try to yell out something else, the level of the music took a sudden dive. We all turned toward the stage. McCully was standing beside the DJ. I guess he'd told him to turn down the volume. A couple of kids booed and hissed. Personally I was grateful. If the music had stayed that loud for the entire dance, I think my ears would have started to bleed. It was still loud, but now I could hear people talking.

"Can you guys excuse me?" David said. "I've got to use the can. I'll be a while because the only washroom in the building big enough for my chair is at the far end of the school." We watched as David rolled away and quickly vanished in the crowd.

"I'm surprised to see you here," Scott said.

"I'm surprised to see you, too."

"You wouldn't be if you'd answered a phone call every now and again. I called to invite you to come, but you weren't in. I left a message with your mother . . . didn't she tell you?"

"No."

"I guess I shouldn't be that surprised. I don't think she likes me hanging around with you."

"No, I don't think —"

"Don't worry about it. My mother doesn't like me hanging out with *you*."

"She doesn't?"

"She says you're a bad influence."

"Me! What about you?"

Scott laughed. "Do you want something to drink?"

"Yeah, that would be great. I'm dying of thirst."

"Good, come on," Scott said.

"Hold on." I grabbed him by the arm and pointed to the punch bowl. "The drinks are the other way."

"Not the ones we have in mind."

"Who's we?"

"Me and Nick and Gavin. Come on, we have to go outside."

"Why would we need to go outside to get a drink? Let's just get some of the punch."

"I don't want punch. Gavin brought something special."

I gave him a questioning look and he leaned forward. "Beer," he whispered in my ear.

"Beer!" I exclaimed.

"Quiet!" he shushed me. "You can't just blab it out loud. You know how much trouble we'd get in if anybody found out?"

"I've got a pretty good idea. You'd be suspended — for a long time." I paused. "Where did he get the beer from?"

"Gavin snuck a twelve pack out of his house. He stashed it in the bushes behind the gym. Come on, twelve beers divided into four guys is three each."

"That's the best math I've ever heard you do. Now can you divide twelve by three?"

"Sure, that's . . . don't you want to join us for a beer?" Scott asked.

"I've got to wait here for David."

"David? Did you come here with him tonight?"

"Yeah," I mumbled.

"You're taking this hosting stuff way too seriously."

"I don't have any choice. McCully told me to watch him." Then I got an idea of how to explain why Scott hadn't seen me in detention. "As long as

I do a good job taking care of David, I don't get detentions when I do little things wrong." It was strange, but I felt like I was almost embarrassed to admit to Scott that I was being good, like he'd look down on me for not getting in trouble.

"Wow, that is a good deal! Do you think he needs a second guy to help out?"

"I think one is enough. Besides, you only do *big* things wrong, so it wouldn't save you."

"You got a point there," Scott agreed. "So you don't want a beer?"

"No, I got to wait here."

Scott shrugged. "Suit yourself. It just leaves more for me and Nick and Gavin. I'll be back after I've had a couple of brewskis."

Scott left me alone in the middle of the crowded floor. I felt so stupid standing there by myself that for a second I thought maybe I should have gone along. I didn't want to have any beer, but I didn't want to be standing here by myself even more. It seemed like people were looking at me. Maybe I could just go outside and stand with them. I didn't have to drink. I could just be there, joke around, be part of the guys again. I couldn't get in trouble if I didn't drink . . . if I was just there with my friends.

I was about to start for the door when I caught sight of David coming back across the floor. He wasn't alone — Caroline and Lisa were walking with him.

"Look who I ran into," David said. They both said hello to me and I mumbled back. "Where'd Scott go?" David asked.

"He went outside," I answered, without volunteering what he was doing there.

"It's good that he left," David said.

"It is?"

"Yep, if he'd have stayed, it would have been three guys and two girls. Uneven numbers for dancing."

"Dancing?"

"Yes, this is a dance, remember? What do you say that the four of us go out and dance?" David suggested.

"But nobody is dancing." I motioned to the small open spot by the front that was now completely deserted. Even the group of girls had given up.

"Nobody is dancing *yet*. They need somebody to get it started, and we're definitely four somebodies."

Neither of the two girls looked any more thrilled than I did.

"I don't know —"

"Come on, don't be such a suck," David interrupted. "It's not like I'm asking you to jump out of an airplane."

I would have rather jumped out of a plane. That would have been much less scary.

"Nobody will die," David said.

Could somebody die of embarrassment? I wondered.

"Come on."

David rolled across the gym and the three of us reluctantly followed. He stopped at the front, right in the very middle of the dance floor, and I stood beside him and the two girls faced us. David started moving his upper body in time to the music, and the girls started to move, just a little, but enough to show they were dancing. I looked at the crowd of people who were standing all around the dance floor. This time it wasn't just my imagination — all eyes were on us.

"Come on, Sean, it's easy. Do what I do," David said seriously. "Just watch my footwork." Then he burst into laughter and the tension I knew the three of us were feeling evaporated.

I started to shuffle my feet. Caroline flashed me a big smile and I smiled back. I tried to watch how she was moving her arms and imitate it.

"That's the way," David said.

As we continued to dance, we were joined on the floor. First by a few girls, and then a boy and girl, and then another couple, and another. Soon we were in the middle of a cluster of kids on the dance floor. I felt more protected and loosened up my arms and legs. Maybe I didn't dance too bad after all . . . and maybe this whole thing wasn't too bad, either. I looked over at David, moving to the music, a smile on his face, and he looked back at me and winked.

Chapter 8

"And don't talk to him like he can't hear or is stupid just because he's in a wheelchair!" I said emphatically.

"Why would we do that?" my mother asked.

"I don't know, but people seem to do it."

I had finally asked David why people talked slower and louder to him, and he said that sometimes people thought that because his legs didn't work, neither did his brain or ears. I'd wondered if I had ever done that, and he said no, and that, if I had, we wouldn't have become friends.

And then I remembered something else. "Whatever you do, don't push his chair around. It isn't a stroller."

"I don't care if it is a stroller," my father said as he clicked off the TV to silence the football game.

"Ever since Julia and Jamie outgrew their twin stroller, I'm through pushing anything — at least until the grandchildren arrive." He smiled broadly.

"Funny, very funny. Just don't push his chair even if you think you're helping him."

"We wouldn't dream of it," my mother replied. "I hope you don't mind that I invited him for dinner. It's just that he was coming over anyway to work on that project you two are doing, so I thought it was only polite."

"It's not a problem," I said, hoping that I was right because I knew David *could* be a problem.

I'd known him only a few weeks, and it wasn't like I was around him all the time, but I'd seen his temper flare a dozen times. And when he lost it, it happened fast. One second he'd be okay, even happy and joking around, and then somebody would say something, or maybe it was the *way* they said something, and he'd just go off. Half the time I didn't even knew what had set him off.

And it wasn't just with kids our age that he was like that. Twice he'd jumped down the throat of a teacher. He had said things that would have caused me to be sent straight down to the office — and maybe home under suspension. But he got away with it.

"I don't see what you're so worried about. I wasn't this nervous the first time I brought a girl-friend home to meet my parents," my father said.

"I'm not nervous!" I protested.

"Everything will be fine, dear," my mother reassured me.

"It's just that, you know, with him being in the chair some things are different. I want him to feel welcome."

"Don't worry about that. You've been friends with David for three weeks, and we haven't even heard from your school. As far as I'm concerned, he's welcome to move in with us!" My father laughed loudly.

"Sean's friend is going to move in?" Julia asked.

"He can stay in our room with us," Jamie added.

"He's not moving in. Dad's just joking around." I turned to my mother. "Couldn't you feed them supper now and send them to bed?"

"No way we're going to bed early!" Jamie stuck her chin in the air and crossed her arms.

"That's not fair!" Julia agreed. "We're not babies, we're big girls!"

"You're not big girls, you're only four!" I argued.

"Regardless, they're too old to go to bed at six o'clock," my father chimed in.

"Don't worry, girls. You'll eat with us, but get to your bath and bed maybe a bit earlier than usual," Mom said. "Now, you two need to go and wash up a little before company comes."

As they left the room they were almost bowled

over by our older sister, Janice.

"Gotta go!" she yelled as she headed for the front door.

"Don't forget about your curfew!" Dad called out.

"How can I forget about it? All my friends have a later curfew, so they'll all still be there to remind me to go home," she said sarcastically.

"We're not responsible for the limits their parents place on them," Mom said.

"Or don't place on them," my father added.

"I'm almost sixteen, and I should be able to stay out later than eleven on a Friday night!"

"How do you figure that ten months shy of your sixteenth birthday makes you *almost* sixteen?" Dad asked.

"Aggggg!" she screamed. "What is the point even talking to you!"

"There's no point. If you'd like, though, you can stay in and argue until it's eleven o'clock. At least that way you're guaranteed to be in on time."

"I just wish you two would stop treating me like a baby, like I can't do anything for myself! I want to be independent!" She crossed her arms across her chest and scowled at them. "Well?"

"Well what?" my father asked.

"Isn't somebody going to give me a drive?"

"I'll drive you," Dad offered, "if it wouldn't take away too much of your independence."

"I'll meet you at the car," Janice huffed and

slammed the door behind her.

Mom and Dad burst into laughter.

"You really shouldn't tease her," Mom said.

"I couldn't resist. Besides, you laughed too. I'll be back soon," Dad said and gave Mom a kiss on the cheek.

Janice and my parents always seemed to be fighting or arguing over something. It hadn't been good for a while, but had gotten a lot worse since the move. I'd overheard my parents talking one night about how they'd been "too easy" on her and weren't going to "make the same mistake" with me. I didn't like the sound of that.

"Can you finish setting the table while I check on supper?" Mom asked.

It was almost completely done, with the place-mats, plates, and glasses all in place. I opened the buffet drawer and took out the cutlery. The only way I could ever remember where the utensils went was because "fork" and "left" both have four letters and "knife" and "right" both have five. I put them out at each setting. Next I took the chair away from where David was going to sit. I brought it right out of the room and hid it away in a kitchen corner. Then I checked the ramp I'd set up on the back step. It would be easier for David to come to the back door than to deal with the stairs at the front.

Despite what I'd said to my parents, I was feeling nervous. It wasn't like me and David hadn't eaten a meal together — we hadn't missed a lunch together for the last two weeks. Most of the time we were joined by Caroline and Lisa and Christina. Sometimes some other seveners, their friends, would also be there. Other times, some of the grade eights would sit down with us.

I guess the only thing that really worried me about David coming over was my father — or, I guess, what my father might say. It wasn't that he was a bad guy. Actually, he was one of the best guys I knew, but sometimes he didn't think about what he was saying. It was like he didn't even know what was going to come out of his mouth until he heard it with his own ears.

There was a knock at the front door and I hurried to answer it, wondering who it could be. I pulled open the door. It was David.

"What are you doing here?" I asked in shock.

"You invited me. Remember?"

"Of course. It was just the stairs . . ."

"There are stairs?" he asked.

"Yes, there are stairs . . ." I let the sentence fade away as I realized he was kidding.

"I got up them. It can be done," David explained.

I then noticed the scuff marks on his pants. Once before I'd seen him get out of his chair and pull himself up a set of stairs, dragging the chair up after him and then climbing back up into it.

"It's just that the back door only has one step . . . and . . . and I set up a ramp."

"A ramp? That was nice, but I like coming in the front door," David said.

At that instant Julia and Jamie came roaring into the room.

"So are these your little sisters?"

"Yep, these are the Boo Boos."

"I'm telling Mommy," Julia threatened.

I wasn't supposed to call them that anymore. "Okay, okay. David, this is Julia and Jamie."

David reached out his hand. "Pleased to meet you, girls." They both reached out and awkwardly shook.

"Nice chair," Jamie said.

"Thank you."

"Could I have a turn in it?" Julia asked.

"Julia! It's not a —"

"That's okay," David said, cutting me off. "You can't have a turn, but I will take you for a ride if you want."

"Me, too!" Jamie squealed.

"Of course. Both of you climb up and I'll take you for a spin."

They yelled with delight and scrambled onto his lap. I wondered if it hurt to have them poking and digging into him . . . or whether he could even feel it at all.

"Where to, girls?" David asked.

"Our room!" Julia screamed. Their bedroom, like everything else in our bungalow, was on the same floor.

"Tell me where to go," David said and he pushed off down the hall with them yelling out directions for him to "go faster."

As they disappeared down the hall, Mom came in from the kitchen. "Who was at the door?"

"David."

"But I thought he'd have to come in through the back door."

"So did I."

"Where is he now?" my mother asked.

"He's just being given a tour of the house by the Boo . . . by the girls."

"Call me back when he's through with the tour so I can meet him. Supper's almost ready. We'll eat when your father gets back." She went back into the kitchen.

I decided David had been held prisoner by the Boo Boos long enough and maybe I should rescue him. As I came to their room, David's back was to me, and the two girls were standing in front of him.

"But why don't your legs work?" Julia asked.

My mouth dropped open in shock. I stepped back slightly out of the room. I wanted to hear the answer, but didn't want to be seen.

"I was in an accident."

"What kind of an accident?"

"A car crash."

"Were you driving?" Julia asked.

David laughed. "I'm too young. My father was driving."

"Is he in a wheelchair, too?" Jamie questioned.

"He was hurt . . . but he's okay now," he said in a soft voice.

Without realizing it, the girls had asked the question I wanted to, but didn't have the guts.

"That's good that he can walk now," Julia said loudly.

I didn't want this to go too far. "Supper's almost ready," I said, stepping into the room.

David spun his chair around. "Do you like my new friends?" His lap was filled to overflowing with stuffed animals, including the favorite teddy bears of both my sisters.

"The girls asked if I could give their animals a ride as well."

"If you want," Julia said softly, "you can even keep my teddy bear all through dinner."

David looked at Julia, then up at me, then back to her. "Thanks. I'd like that."

"Have you two finished washing up?" I asked the twins.

"Sort of," Julia said.

"How do you 'sort of' wash up?" I questioned.

"We each washed one hand," Jamie said.

"The one we eat with," Julia added.

I shook my head slowly. "Not good enough. *Both* of you go and wash *both* hands . . . or I'll tell Mom."

They exchanged a look. I knew they also exchanged the same unspoken thought about me bugging them. Without a word they headed off to the bathroom. We headed for the dining room.

"Sean, why are they called the Boo Boos?"

"My older sister is fifteen and I'm thirteen."

"Yeah?"

"So the two of them are nine years younger. You know . . . an afterthought . . . a mistake. They were a boo boo."

* * *

"Could I please have another helping of chicken?" David asked.

"Of course!" my mother beamed. She loved people enjoying her cooking. She piled two more pieces on his plate.

"You can really shovel away the food," Dad said. "You must have a wooden leg!"

There was stunned silence. My father had put his foot into his mouth once again.

"I . . . I . . . meant . . ." he stammered.

"That's okay," David said, interrupting his explanation. "My mother says the same thing."

"David and his family live over on Chambers Avenue," I said, trying to move the conversation away from my father's blunder.

"We looked at a few places on Chambers before we purchased this one," Dad said. I could tell he was grateful to have the topic move someplace else. "There are some very nice houses there."

"It's okay, I guess," David said. "Are you happy with your new place?"

"Yes, but it's smaller than our last home. The twins have to share a room. Moving to the city was more expensive than living where we did, so this was the biggest place we could afford."

"Our place is smaller, too," David said.

"Was your move job related, too?" my father asked.

"No . . . we needed a different type of house, a bungalow."

Of course, the answer to why was obvious. A bungalow meant no steps.

"So what is the project you two are working on?" my father asked.

"It's for science," I answered.

"It's about cell regeneration," David added. "You know, the way some amphibians and reptiles can lose their tails and grow back new ones."

"Sounds interesting," my mother said.

"It is . . . well, for school anyway," I agreed.

"And when is this project due?" she asked.

I knew what she was getting at. Last year I'd had trouble getting things in on time.

"Two weeks from this Monday," David said.

"So you have a lot of time to work on it," she said.

"I just think it's better to get things done early and get them out of the way," David replied.

My parents looked smugly pleased. They'd

been saying that sort of thing to me for years.

"Oh, Sean, I forgot to mention, you had a phone call while you were out shooting hoops on the driveway," Mom said.

"I did? Who called?"

"She said her name was Caroline."

I felt myself start to blush.

"Who's that, Seany?" Julia asked.

"She's just somebody from my school," I mumbled.

"Somebody he was dancing with at the school dance," David added and I shot him the evil eye.

The Boo Boos started to giggle. "Seany's got a girlfriend, Seany's got a girlfriend," they chanted.

My dad smirked. I knew what was going through his head and just hoped it wouldn't come out his mouth.

"Girls, leave your brother alone," my mother finally said.

"Thank you," I said and everybody fell silent.

"I think it's sweet. I remember the first girl I had a crush on," my father said.

"I don't have a crush on anybody! I just danced with her a couple of times and that's all!" I had to get away from this topic. "I made the first basketball cut," I blurted out.

"Wonderful," my father exclaimed. "I'm glad you're not letting yourself be distracted."

"I hardly even know her!" I protested.

"No, no!" Dad said. "I meant with other things

. . . staying out of trouble."

"Oh . . . I understand." Thank goodness.

"How many were cut from the team and how many players are they down to?"

"Nine gone and twenty still trying out."

"How many is he going with?" Dad asked.

"Ten on the team as well as two on a practice squad. Coach wants to be able to run full team practices even if somebody's away."

"Well, forget about the practice squad. You want one of the starting five spots. Just stay aggressive and work on driving to the hole," my father said.

"I'm trying. I've been working on a fade-away hook shot. David showed me how to do it."

"He did?"

"Yeah, it's a good shot," David jumped in, "but I think your dad's right. You have to work on going harder under the net."

"How would you know I need to go harder?" I asked. He'd never seen me play against anybody.

"I watched a couple of the practices."

"You did?"

"Yeah. I sat down by the far end. You've got to stop dishing out the ball so much and take more shots."

"Assists are important, too!" I protested.

"Of course they are, but you pass out too often when you have the ball in the paint. You have to force it up, make them foul you."

"Haven't I been saying the same thing?" my father chipped in. "Take it hard to the hoop and don't be afraid of contact."

"I'm not afraid of contact!"

"Only pass out if they double down on you," David instructed. "Don't be afraid to shoot. Remember you miss all the shots you don't take."

"Sounds like David knows his game," my father said, sounding impressed.

"He does."

"So you like watching basketball," Dad said.

"Not particularly. I like playing the game."

"Are you in a wheelchair league or something?"

"I don't play . . . anymore."

Dad turned his head sideways and looked at David. "You look like a player, but it's hard to tell your height when you're sitting in the chair. How tall did you used to be?"

"I'm the same height I was before the accident," David snapped, and I could see the fire burning in his eyes.

"I didn't mean anything," my dad apologized. I knew that he didn't mean any offense.

"Maybe we better get started on our project," I said.

"Sorry, but you can't do that," Dad said as he rose to his feet. "No homework until you two show me that fade-away hook shot."

David's expression softened and he smiled. We all smiled. The tension dissolved. That was one of the things about my father: no matter where he put his foot, his heart was always in the right place.

Chapter 9

"What do you say we call it quits for the night?" David said.

"We did a lot more than I thought we could in one night," I agreed. "Maybe we can finish it up tomorrow."

"I'm busy all weekend. How about next weekend?" David asked.

"Maybe next Saturday."

"That would be good," David said. "So . . . are you going to give Caroline a call tonight?"

"I don't even know how she got my phone number."

"Maybe she got it from the phone book," David suggested.

"We have an unlisted number."

"Or maybe I gave it to her," he mumbled.

"Maybe?"

"Okay, fine, I gave it to her. She said she wanted to give you a call. You don't mind, do you?"

"No . . . I was just surprised, that's all."

"Why? Didn't you know she likes you?"

"She does?"

"Isn't it obvious?" David asked.

"Nothing about girls is obvious to me at all."

"Girls are like everything else. Practice makes perfect. If you want to understand them, you have to spend time around them. Like at the dance."

"Oh, yeah, did you have to bring that up at the dinner table?"

"I didn't mean to embarrass you."

I thought about the things my father and sisters had said to him. "I'm okay." I paused. "I hope you're okay about things, too."

"What sort of things?"

"You know, my sisters bugging you and some of the things my father said."

"What did your father say?" David asked.

"Wooden leg . . . how tall you were. He doesn't mean any harm. He's a good guy. Really."

"I believe you. It was fun shooting hoops with him after dinner." He paused. "And I liked your little sisters. How did you think they were bugging me?"

"Putting the stuffed animals in your lap."

"That was fun."

"And asking you for rides."

"I didn't mind that at all. What else?"

"All the questions," I said quietly.

"I didn't mind answering their questions. They've probably never met a kid in a wheelchair before."

"That's for sure."

"They were just curious. Sometimes little kids are even afraid of me. It's like anything else. People are afraid of what they don't know." He paused. "How much did you hear?"

I looked away. "Some of it."

"Didn't *you* want to know what happened to me?"

"Yeah," I answered softly. "I just didn't think I should ask."

"It's not like it's a secret that I'm in a chair."

"I know. I just thought you wouldn't want to talk about it . . . what with everything that happened."

It was David's turn to remain silent. "There's nothing I can do about any of it. You just go on . . . that's all."

"I don't know if I could," I admitted.

"You could, because you have to. There isn't any choice. You just keep going."

We lapsed into silence. I didn't think he was right about how I'd handle things. I wasn't like him. David was strong and confident and so . . . so brave. I wasn't necessarily any of those. It wasn't that I was a coward, or weak or anything, but I wasn't like him.

"Is there anything you want to know that your sisters didn't ask?" David questioned.

"What?"

"Questions. Is there anything you want to know about being in a chair?"

"I don't think so," I blurted out.

"Nothing? There must be something. If we're friends you've got to feel comfortable enough to ask me stuff."

"Well . . . I was wondering . . . when my sisters were in your lap . . . were they heavy . . . like, could you feel them?"

"That's more like it. I can feel a little bit. Mostly in the toes of my right foot. I've got what they call patchy spots. Little spots of feeling and sensation are still there, even though I can't move my legs. For the most part there's nothing." David slapped himself hard on the leg and it made a resounding noise. "Can't feel that at all."

"So there's no pain?"

"Not really. Sometimes I think I feel something, but I really don't. It isn't like when somebody has a leg or arm taken off. Those people can have what's called phantom pain. Their brain tells them that they have an ache where they don't even have a limb anymore. Pretty eerie, isn't it?"

"Definitely," I agreed.

"Nerves can be strange that way. It's like the things we've been working on in our project."

"Newts growing back their tails?"

"Yeah, there's lots of overlap. It involves nerves and the way bodies work. Do you know anything about spinal cords?"

"Not really."

"They're sort of like the highway for information to travel back and forth between your body and your brain. When the spine gets injured, the information doesn't flow and things stop working."

"And your spine got injured."

"My L5 vertebrae got crushed. I guess I was lucky it wasn't higher up the spine."

"What do you mean?"

"The farther up, the more you lose. If the break is up by the neck, you become a quad— no movement in any of the four limbs. If it's right at the top of the neck, you can't even breathe or talk on your own."

"You know a lot about this stuff."

"Wouldn't you if you were me? I study everything I can get my hands on."

"Is it hard to find information?" I asked.

"Getting it is no problem. Understanding it is the difficult part. It's all written by scientists and doctors and researchers, and they're not writing for kids. But that hasn't stopped me from learning all I could learn."

I laughed.

"What's so funny?" David asked.

"It's just that I can't picture anything stopping you."

"You're right about that. This can slow me down, but it isn't going to stop me. Someday I'll get out of this chair and walk again."

"You will?"

"Yes I will," he said. His voice was calm but distant, and his face hardened into an angry gaze. "I won't be spending the rest of my life in this chair. I don't know when, but I know it will happen!"

There was an uneasy silence. I think David was as surprised by what he said as I was. He was looking down intently at the desk and our work.

"David . . ."

He looked up.

"I believe you."

He smiled.

Chapter 10

I opened my locker and rummaged around for the books I'd need for the first part of the day.

"Hey, man, how's it going?"

It was Scott. "What are you doing here so early?" I asked.

"Morning detention."

"That's strange."

"No stranger than my math teacher. I'm already booked for after-school detentions for the next week and a half, so he told me to show up this morning. It's hard when you're such a popular guy."

I laughed. "Some things don't change."

"I guess not . . . but some things do. It's not just that I don't see you in detention or class. I don't see you at all," Scott said.

"I can't help how they schedule classes," I said, turning back toward my locker to search for my books so I wouldn't have to look him in the eyes.

"I don't just mean classes. How about after school?"

"You know I have basketball tryouts."

"I mean later. You haven't gone anywhere with me and the guys."

"I've been pretty busy," I explained.

"But not too busy for your friend David. Like I know you're his host and it's keeping you out of trouble with McCully, but you shouldn't forget your old friends."

"I haven't forgotten anybody," I protested. Not forgetting was actually the problem. I remembered all the problems we got into too well.

"Yeah, yeah, yeah. Talk is cheap. We're going to the new roller rink Friday night. Why don't you come with —"

"Hi, Sean!"

I recognized Caroline's voice and turned around so quickly I almost bumped my head on the corner of the locker door.

"Hi, Caroline!" She was standing with Christina and Lisa. It seemed like they were always together.

Scott scowled at them. I don't know what bothered him more, being interrupted or looking at seveners. I'd heard he'd started to give some of the grade sevens a real hard time.

He turned back to me. "Are you going to come with us or what?"

"Come where?" Caroline asked.

Scott's scowl grew, and as he opened his mouth to say something, something nasty I was sure, I jumped in. "To the roller rink on Friday."

"We went last weekend," Lisa said.

"It was really fun," Caroline confirmed. "We may go again."

"Whatever," Scott said, dismissing them. "So are you going to come with us or what?"

"I don't know," I said. It would be fun. It was always fun hanging with Scott and the guys. At least fun until the inevitable trouble began. But then again, trouble at the roller rink wasn't going to cause problems for me at school. A night out with the guys might be just what I needed.

"Sure, I'll come."

Scott smiled and slapped me on the back. "Great! It'll be just like old times! I better get going. I don't want to be late for detention . . . being late is how I got it in the first place." He ambled down the hall, making the other kids move out of his way.

"Maybe we'll see you there," Caroline said.

"What?" I asked.

"At the roller rink, Friday. We'll probably go," she said and the other two girls giggled.

"Um, I'm not even positive I'm allowed to go." Especially if my parents found out that Scott was going to be there.

"You really should go," Christina said. "You can even bring your own roller blades. Do you have blades?"

"Yeah," I answered, although I really wasn't very good on them and didn't use them much.

"We better get going," Caroline said. "Our first class is on the far side of the school. See you at lunch."

Watching them walk away, I felt even more confused. I knew I shouldn't go, but I felt almost a magnetic attraction to the rink. And it would be okay to spend time with my old friends. I had missed them. And the girls being there would be okay, too.

I didn't even know why, but I thought it was best not to mention any of this to David. There was no point in rubbing it in, talking about things he couldn't be a part of.

* * *

Dad pulled the car up to the curb in front of the rink. There was a steady flow of traffic and kids walking along the sidewalk and up to the front doors.

"What time should I be back to get you?" Dad asked.

"It's over at ten. I don't know if I'm going to stay for it all. How about I give you a call around eight?"

"That would be fine." He paused and looked at me strangely. "You never mentioned who you were going with tonight."

"There's a lot of kids going from my school," I answered. I knew how he'd react if I told him it was Scott and the guys I'd be with. Even worse would be the kidding I'd get if he thought I was going to meet Caroline and her friends. They'd mentioned at lunch again that they might be coming here tonight.

"There's nothing to be embarrassed about."

"Embarrassed?" I asked.

"I wasn't born old, you know, Sean. I assume that young lady you like . . . what's her name?"

"Caroline," I answered before I could stop myself.

"Yes, Caroline. Isn't she going to be here tonight?"

I felt myself blush. "She might be. Lots of people might be."

He chuckled softly and reached over and placed a hand on my shoulder. "It's perfectly natural for somebody your age to like girls. There's more to life than basketball and school."

"There is?" I asked in amazement.

"Here, take this," he said, stuffing something into the pocket of my shirt.

I reached in and pulled it out. It was two folded-up five-dollar bills. This was getting more confusing all the time.

"Just in case you need a little extra cash . . . to pay for somebody else to get in or to buy them a drink or something." He smiled. "Now get going. I'm holding up traffic and you don't want to keep anybody waiting."

In a daze I climbed out of the car.

"Hold on a second!" my dad called out. "You think you might need these?" He held up my blades. I'd left them on the floor of the car.

"Thanks," I said as I leaned in and took them.

"Have fun!"

I slammed the door closed and he drove off, leaving me to join the crowd going into the arena. I was amazed at how many people there were. Some were my age, a few younger, but most were high school kids. I stopped at the end of the ticket line and slowly shuffled forward. When I found out how much it cost to get in, I was even more grateful for the money my father had given me. Without it I could hardly have afforded to buy myself a drink after paying for my admission.

"Can I see your blades, please?" the attendant asked.

"Sure," I answered, unsure why he'd want to look at them.

He turned them over and spun the wheels with his hands. "These are okay, you can wear them inside."

"What?"

"Your wheels look practically new. They're

clean and they won't mark up our floor, so you can use them instead of renting skates," he explained as he returned them to me.

"Thanks."

I went through the second set of doors and found myself standing right beside the floor rink. The light was dim and a strobe light was shooting out beams of brightness. The music was loud. I was startled by a sudden hissing sound and jumped slightly. A cloud of dry ice spread across the whole floor of the skating area, hiding the feet of the skaters. This was wild. Somehow I thought it was going to be like ice skating at the rink. This was more like a dance, except this time I didn't have David around to take care of me. Actually I had nobody. I was just standing there by myself as people walked and wheeled by. Everybody was with somebody except me.

"Funny meeting you here!" a voice said from behind me.

I turned around and my mouth almost dropped to the ground. It was David!

"What are you doing here!" I exclaimed.

David shook his head. "Think about it, Sean. I'll try and break it down for you in little chunks. This is a roller rink so I'm here to . . ."

"Roller skate?"

"Exactly. Do you like my skates?" he asked, motioning down to his feet, which were in the rests of the wheelchair but clad in shiny black roller blades with bright red wheels.

"You can skate?" I asked in confusion.

"Don't be silly, of course, I can't skate, but I can roll around better than anybody else out there on the floor. After all, practice makes perfect."

"But why are you wearing skates?"

"So I fit in. As long as I'm wearing skates, maybe nobody will notice the chair."

"Um . . . I . . . Um . . ."

"Snap out of it, Sean, that was a joke!"

I nodded my head and tried to smile but felt confused and stupid.

"It's the policy of the roller rink. Nobody is allowed out on the floor who isn't wearing skates. You wouldn't believe the fight I got into with the manager of this place before they agreed to let me go out with everybody else."

Somehow it didn't seem like a big stretch of the imagination to think of David getting into a fight with somebody.

"They told me nobody could go onto the floor without skates, so I told them I'd rent a pair just like everybody else."

"And they agreed?"

"They had no choice. Besides, they should be happy with the arrangement. Here I am paying the same price as everybody else, and I'm not even wearing down the wheels. This is really quite the place, isn't it?"

"I haven't seen much. I just arrived. It sure is big . . . and loud."

"And fancy. I got here about twenty-five minutes ago, so I've had a chance to really check things out. There isn't a single stair in the whole building. Everything is built for wheels and rolling. This place is like heaven for somebody in a chair."

I was going to answer when I saw Scott, Gavin, and Nick approach. They all waved as they saw me, and then I saw Scott's expression change when he spotted David beside me.

"Good to see you, man!" Nick shouted. He turned to Scott. "Told you he'd be here!"

"You owe us both a drink, Scott," Gavin added.

I gave Scott a questioning look.

"I didn't think you'd show. We had a little bet and I lost." He shrugged. "And I guess it's okay that you invited along David."

"He didn't invite me," David replied.

Scott turned to David. "How . . . did . . . you . . . get . . . here?" Scott asked in that slow, loud voice I knew David hated so much. I held my breath, wondering what David was going to say.

"By helicopter," David said.

"I . . . mean . . . who did you come with?" Scott asked.

"Friends," David said. His voice was calm but I saw a look of anger in his eyes. "They're right over there," he said, lifting up his arm and waving to the tables by the snack bar. A group of girls waved back: Caroline, Lisa, and Christina. I was glad to see them but felt embarrassed in front of the guys. I gave a small wave back.

"Sean didn't even know I was going to be here. He was pretty surprised to see me," David continued.

"Nobody can blame him for being surprised," Scott scoffed, speaking more to Nick and Gavin than David. "Everybody in the place must be surprised to see a guy in a wheelchair here!"

"What do you mean by that?" David demanded.

"Well . . . it's not like you can . . . skate or anything," Scott said in that same exaggerated voice.

"Scott —" I started to say when David raised a hand to silence me.

"Hey, the man's got a point," David said. "Me being here probably makes as much sense as him being in school. Except, of course, there's a much better chance I'll get up and skate than there is of him actually learning anything. If you'll excuse me, I've got to get back to my friends." David turned abruptly and left as Gavin and Nick started to snicker.

"You can really be a jerk sometimes," I snapped.

"What did I say?" Scott questioned.

"Can somebody explain it to him? Maybe if you use small words he'll understand," I said. I shook my head and walked away. David and the girls didn't even notice me coming. They were all talking and laughing.

"Hi, everybody," I said.

"You want to squeeze in here at the table?" Caroline asked.

I felt my face flush.

"There's plenty of space," David said. "Just another one of the advantages of me bringing my own seat with me everywhere."

"Um, maybe I'll join you later. I just came over to say hello."

"Just as well. I don't think we're going to sit around anyway. Do you girls want to hit the floor?"

They all answered enthusiastically.

"You coming out with us?" David asked.

I held up my blades. "It's not just you who has to wear skates before going out on the floor. I'll see you later."

I watched them glide out onto the floor and join the kids already skating to the music. I'd find the guys, put on my skates, and go out. Once I was on the floor there was no telling who I was with . . . and who I wasn't with.

* * *

Roller blading was fun. I'd called my dad to tell him I was going to stay to the end. He'd asked me if I'd used the money he gave me. I used some of it to buy a couple of drinks for myself. Blading could really work up a sweat — at least, if you were using them instead of just wearing them. Scott and Gavin and Nick spent most of the time on the sidelines, watching people and making snide remarks to each other. A couple of times they disappeared into the washroom to have a smoke, even though there were big signs all over the place that said "No Smoking."

I spent some time sitting with them on the benches at the side, but there was no way I was going to hang out in a washroom. So when they left, I felt free to join David and the girls. They were easy to find. They were always on the floor, moving to the music, talking and laughing and having a good time. That was the biggest difference between the two groups: they were really enjoying themselves, while the guys were working hard at *pretending* they were having fun. They could pretend all they wanted and smoke their lungs out for all I cared. I was going out to skate some more. I had made only a few circuits of the floor when the song ended and the DJ came on the P.A.

"The next song is a moonlight skate for couples only . . . moonlight skate for couples only. All others please leave the floor."

As the lights dimmed even lower, I joined one of the lines of people trying to exit the floor. There was a tap on my shoulder. I turned around to see

Caroline.

"Sean, do you want to skate?"

"I'd like to, but it's a couple's skate only."

"I meant with me," she said. "You know . . . the two of us would make a couple."

"Oh, yeah," I stammered. What an idiot I am! "That would be okay."

Caroline reached out and took my hand as the music started. We began to skate. I wondered if my hand was sweaty from all the skating. There weren't that many people on the rink and I felt very visible. What sort of comments from the guys was this going to cost me?

We skated very quickly, completing a lap of the nearly empty skating surface. Slowly other couples filtered out. We hadn't said a word since she first took my hand, and I thought I should say something . . . try to talk.

"Are you having fun tonight?" I asked. Not the brightest question in the world but the best I could come up with. Somehow holding her hand made my brain feel numb.

"A really good time. Even better than the last time. David is so much fun."

I looked around the floor. Where was David? "I'm surprised he isn't out here with Lisa or Christina," I said.

"Lisa asked him but he said he had something important to do."

"Important?" I asked.

"That's what he said, but he didn't tell us what it was, just took off really fast."

"He didn't go home, did he?"

"No, he said he'd be back in a few minutes," she answered. "I wanted to ask more but he got that . . ." She let her sentence trail off.

"He got what?" I asked.

"This is stupid. I shouldn't even be talking about it . . . it's just me being silly."

"Oh, go on, tell me."

There was a pause. "It's just this look he gets in his eyes."

I laughed.

"I told you it was silly." She started to blush.

"No, that's not why I'm laughing. I know exactly what you mean. I've seen it. It's almost . . . now you'll think I'm being stupid."

"No, I won't. Honest," she said.

"It's almost scary."

She nodded her head. "I'm glad it isn't just me who sees it." She sounded relieved and flashed me a big smile. Now it was my turn to blush.

The hand that Caroline wasn't holding suddenly felt sweaty, and I rubbed it on the leg of my pants. I couldn't think of any way to wipe off the other hand. My only hope was that she'd think it was *her* hand that was sweating. We did a few more laps in silence. This was an unbelievably long song. Was it ever going to end?

As we started to turn for yet another lap, I

caught sight of a commotion off to the side. Caroline had noticed it, too, and as we started the other way we both tried to crane our necks back to get a look, but it was no good. Without exchanging a word, we had the same idea and cut the next end short so we could see what was happening. We skated back toward the action, which was moving along the sidelines in our direction.

"It's Scott!" I exclaimed. A couple of big roller rink staff had him and Nick and Gavin by the arms. Still holding Caroline's hand, I slowed down and led us through one of the exits off the floor. I didn't know what was happening, but I wanted to find out. As we watched, the guys were escorted toward the door, shoes in hand, and kicked out of the building!

"Wow, I wonder what they did?" Caroline asked.

"Could have been almost anything, knowing them."

"That Scott guy is really a jerk," Caroline said.

"No, he's . . ." I stopped. Why was I arguing? She was right. "Sometimes he is."

"Why do you hang around with him then?"

"We don't really spend that much time together," I answered truthfully. I felt grateful that she wasn't at Homelands last year to know that Scott and I were practically joined at the hip.

I spotted David moving through the crowd. He had a gigantic smile pasted on his face. I looked down and realized I was still holding Caroline's hand. I tried to let go casually so she wouldn't notice.

"You two looked pretty good out there," David said.

"All right, I guess," I answered, feeling embarrassed all over again. "Did you see them throwing out Scott and Gavin and Nick?"

"Yeah, I had the best seat in the house," David answered. His smile got even wider. "Just before they got caught I was chatting with the security people. Can you believe it, some people can't read and smoke in the washroom?"

"You didn't?" I asked, shocked, although of course I knew he had. He'd been the one who'd turned them in.

"That was really fun. I took up a spot right beside the washroom and got a good look at the whole thing. What a hoot!" David started to laugh. "I . . . guess . . . some . . . people . . . aren't . . . very . . . bright," he said, and I instantly knew why he had done it.

"I'm thirsty. I had no idea that ratting somebody out could work up such a thirst."

"I could use a drink, too," I said. "How about if I treat everybody?" David and Caroline readily agreed. As we rolled over to the snack bar, I realized it would use up the last of the money my father had handed me, but, after all, that's what he gave it to me for.

Chapter 11

I saw Scott coming along the hall. He bumped past a couple of kids. There was no mistaking his actions or expression. He was angry. I wondered what he was so mad about, then it struck me. He was mad at me! I'd stayed inside after he and the guys were turfed out of the roller rink, and then I hadn't even returned his call Sunday. I really didn't want to get into it. Then again, maybe the best defense was a good offense.

"Why did you take off and leave me at the roller rink?" I demanded angrily as he approached.

His expression changed from anger to confusion. "Leave you?"

"Yeah, you invited me to the roller rink and I turn around and you guys are just gone. What's the big idea of ditching me?"

"We didn't ditch you. Don't you know what happened?" he questioned.

"All I know is that you three just bugged out on me."

"It wasn't our idea to leave," Scott said.

"Then whose was it?" I asked, feigning innocence.

"The roller rink security staff. They booted us out."

"You're kidding! What did you do?"

"We were caught smoking in the washroom."

I laughed out loud, pleased with how genuine it sounded, like it was the very first time I'd heard about it.

"So you didn't take off on me?" I said.

"No, but we did wait for you outside for over thirty minutes. We thought you knew we'd been tossed and would come out and join us."

"I would have if I'd known," I lied.

"I guess it was hard for you to notice us getting tossed because your eyes were someplace else."

"What do you mean?" I asked, hoping he wasn't going to say what I thought he was going to say.

He smirked. "Oh, nothing . . . just wondering about you and a couple of seveners, that's all. That reminds me. Where can I find David?" He suddenly looked angry again.

"I don't know," I said. Of course, I knew exactly where he was.

"Aren't you his keeper? Aren't you always

supposed to know where he is so he won't get lost?" Scott asked.

"I'm his host, but he doesn't need my help to find his way around," I said. "Why are you looking for him?"

"Me and him have to have a little *talk* is all."

"About what?"

"About something I heard," Scott said.

He was being deliberately vague. Why wasn't he telling me more, and why was he starting to look even angrier?

"What did you hear?" I asked.

"Look, I don't have time for twenty questions," Scott snapped and took a step to walk away.

I reached out and grabbed him by the arm. "Come on, Scotty, I don't have time for twenty answers, either. Why do you want to talk to him?"

He didn't answer right away and I wondered if he was going to tell me. I let go of his arm.

"I heard from somebody else who was at the roller rink that the guy who turned us in to security was in a wheelchair."

"Who told you that?" I questioned.

"It doesn't matter who. I just know that there was only one guy there in a wheelchair so it had to be him."

I shook my head. "Whoever it is must have heard it wrong. Why would David want to turn you in?"

"I don't know. That's what I want to ask him."

He paused. "And I better like the answer. I got to get going. See you later," Scott said and started back down the hall.

I thought about going after him, but I didn't have time right now. Besides, I knew exactly where David was — at the opposite end of the school, headed for science, the place I was going to now. I looked at my watch. There was less than two minutes to go before the bell sounded. I grabbed my books, slammed the locker door, and clipped on the lock. Not only did I not want to be late, I had to talk to David as soon as possible and warn him about Scott. And, of course if Scott knew, that meant both Nick and Gavin knew as well. They wouldn't be any happier, but they would be less likely to make it into a fistfight.

I hurried along the hall and made it through the door just as the bell sounded and the P.A. clicked to life to begin the announcements.

"Cutting it pretty close, aren't you, Sean?" Mr. Healey, my science teacher, asked as I rushed to my seat in the very back of the class.

I didn't answer but looked over at David sitting in his seat next to me. He nodded at me as I stood up beside him and sang along feebly with the anthem. The announcements followed and I leaned over to David. "Scott knows," I whispered.

"Knows what?" David asked.

"Everything."

"That's quite a change. Last week he didn't

know anything and today he knows everything." He chuckled to himself.

"He knows that you told on him at the roller rink."

"How does he know any of that?" David asked, but judging from the anger in his eyes and the loudness of his voice I suspected he thought it was me.

"I didn't tell him," I said in my defensively. "He said somebody overheard you telling the security guys at the rink. He's looking for you."

"Good."

"Good?"

"Yeah, this day was looking pretty boring."

"If you boys are through talking now, could I start teaching?" Mr. Healey asked.

"Sure . . . sorry," I mumbled.

"Before we go on to new work today, I'd like to give back the research projects you handed in last week," Mr. Healey said. "Many of you will be no more pleased with your marks than I was with your projects. A few are reasonably well done and one is exceptional!"

A few people, those who thought it might be them, sat up straighter in their seats. I didn't have any illusions he was talking about the paper David and I had turned in. It was good — certainly better than the stuff I usually did on my own — but it wasn't "exceptional." The few times I'd pulled off a B was cause for major celebration in my house. If I ever got an A, I'm sure somebody would declare a national holiday.

"This paper went well beyond what was expected or required, and I learned a great deal about the subject myself," he continued.

I hated those brown-nosers who did more than they were supposed to. It made the rest of us look bad, and I didn't need anybody else's help to look bad. I glared at the usual suspects: three kids, including my previous host, Bradley, who all had the strange idea that school was only about learning. Being smart was one thing. Trying to show everybody else that you were smarter than them was another.

Mr. Healey held aloft a paper that looked to be about three times as thick as the one David and I had worked on.

"Could everybody please give David and Sean a round of applause."

David and *Sean*!

There was a smattering of clapping.

"Boys, come on up and get your paper."

David started up to the front and I remained frozen in my seat.

"Come on," David said.

I stumbled to my feet and followed after him.

"Excellent work, boys!" Mr. Healey said as he handed the paper to David.

One of the brainer girls raised her hand. "What did they do it on?"

I wasn't sure if she cared as much as she liked hearing herself talk — you know, the sort of person who asks a question not because they want to hear the answer but to show you how smart they are by asking the question in the first place.

"Regenerating missing body parts, like tails and things," I mumbled in response.

"At least, that was our starting point," David added.

What did he mean "our starting point?" That was our whole paper.

"And then they wrote about the applications for humans, including nerve regeneration," Mr. Healey answered.

"What's that?" somebody else asked.

"It's pretty complicated," David said. He turned to me. "Do you want to try to explain it to them, Sean?" There was a playful look in his eyes.

"Me?" I asked. I couldn't even begin to explain what he was talking about. "No, no, it's . . . it's really complicated . . . maybe they should just read the paper."

"It is complicated, but you did a wonderful job of making it easy to understand," Mr. Healey said. "Perhaps I'll copy the paper and let you all read it."

There was a collective groan from the class.

"Maybe I could explain a little bit about it instead," said David. "It has to do with some scientific research on fixing damaged nerves so they'll work."

He continued to talk and I understood a little of what he was saying from our previous conversations. He was explaining how human nerves and cells die, like skin cells, and are replaced by new cells with new nerves. Judging from the expressions on the faces of the other kids, I was maybe the only one in the whole room beside David and Mr. Healey who had any idea of what he was talking about.

"Boys, we don't have enough time today to do justice to your work," Mr. Healey said. "Instead, how about I hand out the rest of the papers, and you two can give a more full presentation later this week?"

"Sure," I said, anxious to get away from the front of the class, but then realized that I'd agreed to another presentation.

We took our seats as Mr. Healey continued to call out names and pairs of people headed to the front to get their papers back. I leaned over and grabbed the assignment off David's desk and opened it up. There, in a bold red marker, was the grade — A plus! I'd never gotten a mark like that in my life!

I started flipping through the assignment. I found the work we'd done together. It took up the first seven pages. Some illustrations, beautiful illustrations, had been added by David. I continued flipping through the pages until I came to a whole section that was a complete mystery to me. This was the stuff Mr. Healey was so impressed with. It went on for another eight pages and included more of David's art work.

I looked over at David.

"I told you I'd finish it off," he whispered. "Congratulations."

"Congratulations to you," I whispered back. "We have to do a presentation about this. But . . . "

"Don't worry. I'll explain it all to you," he answered.

"How about at lunch?"

"Don't you have other things you want to talk about at lunch . . . with other people?" David broke into a goofy grin and I couldn't help but smile back. I just assumed we'd be eating lunch with Caroline and her friends today, like usual.

"Maybe they'd be interested, too," I said.

David shook his head. "It isn't that interesting. Besides, some of it is kind of personal. Not the sort of thing I want to talk to everybody about."

"Boys, do you think you could put a lid on it, or do I have to lower that mark?" Mr. Healey asked.

"We'll shut up," I said quickly.

Mr. Healey finished handing out the papers and started into his lesson, and I, of course, drifted out. I had other things on my mind. Things like getting an amazing mark, but with David having done most of the work. And what did he mean about the project being very "personal?"

I leaned over closer to David. "Then how about explaining it to me after school?" I whispered.

"What about basketball?"

"Canceled tonight. Coach told us there's a staff meeting he has to go to at three-thirty."

"Okay, after school it is."

I did want to hear about the project, but I wanted to stay close to him in case Scott found him and decided he needed to do more than talk. If Scott was going to pull anything, it would most likely happen today on the way home. I knew Scott well enough to know that he could get pretty mad, but he didn't stay mad for long. If I could keep an eye on David for the next couple of days, the whole thing would blow over.

At least I hoped.

* * *

David and I didn't share the last class of the day, and his locker was at the far end of the school from mine, so we agreed to meet at the front door. I figured even Scott wouldn't be dumb enough, or angry enough, to try to fight him right in the hall. And it was the only door in the school equipped with a ramp. Even if they did meet inside and agreed to "take it outside," David would have to come out that door.

I walked down the incline and took a seat on the edge of the ramp — right where I'd been sitting that first morning when David had taken those shots at me. I nodded or said hello to kids as they filtered past me on their way home. They included guys trying out for the basketball team, kids from my different classes, and even some of the grade sevens I'd gotten to know at the dance and at lunch times. It felt so much better than last year when I hardly knew anybody, and the people I did know were the ones it was probably best not to.

The rush of kids out the doors slowed to a trickle. It was no surprise that David wasn't one of the first out. It wasn't that he couldn't move fast — when we were moving down the hall together I had to work to keep up with him — but that he didn't ever seem to be in a rush. Even when we left a class, he always seemed to wait until everybody else had left before he'd head for the door. But he was taking even longer than usual . . . maybe he'd run into Scott.

"Hey, didn't I already talk to you about being on the wheelchair ramp?"

I jumped to my feet as David rolled down the slope. I looked behind him. Scott was no place to be seen.

"That's better. If you'd gotten out my way that fast the first time, I never would have popped you."

"Then you never would have had the pleasure of having me as your host," I shot back.

"And maybe I would have had some cute girl

show me around instead."

I picked up my pack, threw it over my shoulder, and fell in beside David as he rolled down the sidewalk. "Want to stop by my place for a snack and some hoops?" I asked.

"Can't. I've got a doctor's appointment."

"You sick?"

"Nope. I've got to go to the doctor all the time. It's just part of being in the chair."

We came to a stop at the curb. Cars and trucks whizzed by in a steady stream. A bus brushed by us, and I turned my head as a wave of small stones pelted against my face. I heard a thump and turned back to see David bounce down the curb and into oncoming traffic. In wide-eyed shock I took a half-step forward to follow but pulled back as a truck came barreling along behind the bus. It slowed down and laid on the horn as David cleared the first lane, then it swooshed by between us, blocking him from my view for a split second. He continued across the busy street with vehicles racing by him on all sides. He was going to get hit for sure! Some of the cars slowed down or switched lanes. Finally he cleared the far lane, bumping up onto the other sidewalk. He spun around and motioned for me to cross just as another bus came rolling along the curb lane. Behind it were a few cars and then there was a gap in traffic. I raced across the first three lanes and froze on the center yellow line, waiting for the vehicles to pass in the other direction. The light in the distance changed to red, and, after the last car passed, I crossed over to David.

"What were you doing, waiting for a crossing guard?" he asked.

"It beats waiting for an ambulance," I shot back. "You came close to getting hit a few times."

"Close doesn't count. So, do you still want to hear about nerve regeneration in humans or talk about the best way to cross the street?"

"Regeneration. I have to know enough to fake my part in the presentation."

"I'll see what I can do. I hope you don't mind me adding on to the paper."

"Yeah, I'm really upset. I hate getting good marks."

He smiled.

"But why did you do it without telling me or asking me to work on it with you?"

"I don't know. I was just finishing it up, like we agreed, you know, adding some illustrations, and then I started thinking about how the stuff I know about nerve regeneration fit in so well, so . . . I just kept working. The next thing I knew it was three in the morning and the paper was finished. Let me tell you about what I wrote. You know the body is always repairing itself, right?"

"Like we talk about in the paper — new skin, growing hair, and nails."

"Sure, but other things. Like the way your

body can repair a broken bone."

"Okay, sure."

"But it's more than that. You get a cut or scrape, and it heals over as good as new. Did you know your entire outer layer of skin falls off and is replaced every two weeks?"

"That sounds gross."

"Not as gross as if it didn't get replaced." He paused. "So the body has the ability to repair and replace some parts. Understand?"

I nodded.

"But most parts you can't replace. It's not like an amphibian growing back a tail. If you lose a finger, it doesn't grow back . . . at least not yet," David said.

"Not yet?"

"That's what I said. We can't grow back a finger, yet, but we will be able to."

"Come on, this isn't Star Trek. Get real."

"I am getting real," David insisted. "And not just fingers. I'm talking everything! Let's say a guy's heart doesn't work, or his liver is shot, or he needs new lungs because he gets a disease. So the doctors take a little sample of that part of the body and, bang, they grow him a new one!"

"You've definitely been watching too much science fiction."

"I'm not talking science fiction. I'm talking science fact. Right now that's what's being worked on. Do you understand what nerves are?"

"Yeah — mine practically snapped watching you cross that street."

"Funny. Nerves are the part of your body that communicate information. But sometimes things happen to those nerves, old age or disease . . . or accidents."

I knew what he was talking about. Like the car accident that had crushed his spine and stopped his legs from working. That was why this was so personal.

"And they can regrow those nerves?" I asked.

"In lab experiments they've been able to. It's just a matter of time until they can do it with people. And then they'll be able to regrow the damaged part of my spine and then I'll be able to walk again," David said.

He suddenly stopped his chair and spun around to face me. "I'll stand up and my legs will work again and I'll be able to do everything that everybody else can do. Instead of just watching you play basketball, you and I can be on the same team."

"That would be great!" I said.

"Yeah, great," he said distractedly, and he suddenly stopped talking and looked really intense. "What are you staring at!" he yelled.

"I was just —" I started to answer.

"Not you," David spat out. "I'm talking to those idiots!" he said, pointing a finger at a couple of older teenagers who were walking toward us.

They were in high school for sure and were bigger than us.

"What are you two baboons looking at?" David yelled.

They stopped in their tracks and turned to each other. They looked as confused as I was by his onslaught and didn't answer.

"I'm in a chair, that doesn't mean I'm blind. I saw what you were doing!" David continued.

"What are you talking about, kid?" one of them asked in astonishment.

"I saw you making fun of me!"

"I wasn't doing anything at all."

"I saw the way you were moving your hands like you were in a wheelchair."

"Are you crazy?"

"Who are you calling crazy?" David demanded.

They both looked increasingly uneasy. I noticed a couple of people partway up the block had stopped and were staring at us.

"You're both stupid, ugly liars!" David yelled.

What was he doing picking a fight with these two? I wanted to say something, but I was shocked into silence, as were the two other boys.

"What's wrong, are you guys too stupid to talk?" David demanded.

"Kid, you better shut up!" one of them blurted out, breaking the trance.

"And if I don't, what are you going to do about it?"

"I'll shut you up," the bigger of the two answered. "You and your friend!"

His friend! I hadn't said a word!

"We're not afraid of you!" David replied.

The big guy took a step toward David, and I knew it was going to come to blows. Suddenly, the guy was grabbed from behind by his friend.

"Come on, man, cool it."

"I'm not cooling anything! Somebody's got to do something about his smart mouth," he said as he struggled to free himself from the grip of his friend.

"You can't take a swing at him. He's just a kid in a wheelchair."

He stopped struggling and relaxed. "You're right, I can't smack a kid in a chair . . . but there's nothing to stop me from popping that kid," he said, pointing at me.

"What did I do?" I demanded.

"Leave him alone!" David yelled.

"Yeah, he didn't do anything," the smaller and more reasonable of the two said. "Let's just forget it and get out of here. We're late."

The first nodded his head in agreement, and they started to walk away. As they moved past us, the bigger guy deliberately bumped into me.

"Hey!" I said, spinning around.

"You got a problem?" he demanded. "'Cause if you do, just bring it on."

I felt a surge of electricity flow through my

body. I'd show him who had a problem, I'd just . . . oh, oh . . . it was happening again. I took a deep breath.

"I don't want to fight," I said.

"That's what I figured. One's a cripple and the other's a coward," he snickered.

I looked down at David, who was seething in anger. I took a deep breath. I wasn't necessarily going to get in the best shot or the most shots, but I *was* going to get in the first shot. Balling up my fist, I landed a punch right in the middle of that jerk's big mouth.

* * *

"That wasn't so bad, was it?" David asked.

"Yes, it was."

"It could have been worse."

"It *would* have been much worse if that car hadn't pulled over," I answered, rubbing the side of my jaw where his hardest blow had landed. There'd only been a couple of punches, the first thrown by me and a couple that we'd each caught, when a car squealed to a stop and a lady got out and yelled and screamed until the two guys took off. She offered to drive us home, but David refused. I figured he was hoping they'd return to continue the fight when she drove off, but they were long gone.

"You've got quite the temper," David said.

"Me! I've got a temper? It wasn't me that got us into that!"

"It wasn't me who threw the first punch," David said.

It was hard to argue with that. "He asked for it!"

"He asked *me* for it, not *you*. He called me a cripple."

"And he called me a coward."

"Yeah, I guess you're right, but you have to watch that temper of yours," David said.

"My temper!" I exclaimed in disbelief.

David chuckled. "Maybe me, too. At least nobody got hurt."

"What are you talking about? My jaw is throbbing like crazy and your eye must hurt."

"Yeah, it's a little sore. Hey, how did you know it was hurting?"

"Because I have eyes. I can see that it's starting to swell up."

"It is? I'm in trouble!" he said as he rushed over to a storefront and tried to see his reflection in the plate-glass window. "This isn't good. It really is swollen."

"What do you expect to happen if you get punched in the face?" I asked.

"But you don't understand! My mom is going to kill me. She says I've got to stop getting hurt so much. She says I'm careless."

"Well, this wasn't careless. It was a fight."

"Even worse. She told me she didn't want to hear about me getting into any more fights."

"How many fights have you been in?" I asked. I now knew of two . . . with a third just waiting to happen.

"I don't know. It's not like I keep count or anything."

What that meant was that he'd been in so many that he *couldn't* keep count.

"And this fight wasn't even my fault," David continued.

My eyes widened in shock. "Just whose fault do you think it was?" I questioned, wondering if he was going to blame me again for throwing the first punch.

"That guy. He was asking for it. You saw what he was doing, making fun of me."

I shook my head. "I didn't see anything."

"Great, just great! How could you miss it?" he demanded.

"I guess I was just talking and not paying attention," I apologized, although I was positive I hadn't seen anything, because nothing had happened.

"So if my mother asks you what happened, what will you say?"

I furrowed my brow. "What happened."

"Thanks for nothing," David snapped. The look on his face was a jumble of anger and hurt. Anger I could deal with, I was even used to it from him, but hurt was harder.

I took a deep breath. "And what happened was that we were walking along, minding our own business, when these two goofs bumped into us and started to make fun of you, and then one of them took a poke at me, and we had to fight back. And anybody who didn't see it that way is nothing but a liar."

David reached out and for a split second I wondered if he was going to take a swing at me, but then I realized he just wanted to shake hands. In that instant of hesitation, I looked into his eyes and saw the person I knew — the person I was starting to like better all the time.

Chapter 12

The gym was filled with guys warming up. I looked at the big clock over the bleachers. I had seventeen minutes before Coach showed up at four and things officially began. The sounds of bouncing balls and squeaking sneakers were mixed with good-natured yelling and laughter. I'm always amazed at how some people can be so relaxed about this — for me, there was nothing here that wasn't completely serious. I nodded or said a few hellos to different guys as I slipped off to one of the side baskets to work on a few things.

I took a couple of shots to warm up before getting down to business. As I retrieved the last rebound, I saw David peeking in through the double doors at the far end of the gym. I waved and he waved back. I was surprised when he rolled into the gym and came toward me. I noticed how some of the players stopped shooting to watch him cross the floor.

"I thought you were heading home," I said.

I'd been keeping a pretty close watch on David, and, so far, he and Scott hadn't connected. Scott usually had a detention after school, so as long as David left when classes ended, there was little chance of them meeting at the front doors or on the way home. I'd spoken to Gavin and Nick and convinced them that it wasn't David who turned them in and they were cool with everything. But Scott wasn't going to be convinced.

"I just looked in as I was passing by. You still having problems with that guy?" David asked, pointing to a player at the basket at the far end of the gym.

"Some."

"He's big. Is he strong as well?"

"Very strong," I admitted.

He nodded. "You can't just push on him. You have to alternate. Push really hard and then suddenly move over. He'll fall down like somebody shot him."

"Do you think he's my biggest competition?"

"I haven't watched enough to know," David said.

"Do you think you could?" I asked.

"Could what?"

"Stick around and watch the practice. Then afterward you could tell me things. You know, what I'm doing wrong or tips about other people's games."

He hesitated. "And you won't get ticked off if I tell you things you don't want to hear?"

"Of course not . . . well, not for long anyway." We both laughed.

My laughter stopped short when I saw Scott enter the gym. What was he doing here? He was talking to somebody in the bleachers. He caught sight of me, nodded slightly, and then started in my direction. Why didn't he have a detention and, more important, why was he here? Was he looking for me . . . or looking for David? This was the last place in the world I wanted things to happen.

"How's it going, Scott?" I asked. I needed everything to stay cool. I'd even called his house a couple of times to try to talk to him. It was his turn not to return calls. I wondered if his mother had given him my messages. Maybe she really did think I was a bad influence.

"Things are okay," he answered and then stepped by so he was standing right in front of David.

"You and I need some words," he said angrily to David.

"About what?" David demanded.

"About something I heard you did."

"I do lots of things," David said. His voice was calm and almost casual.

"The roller rink. I heard you turned us in."

"I heard that, too," David replied.

"You did?" Scott asked.

"I told him," I explained, jumping in. "But there's always people talking, spreading rumors. It doesn't mean it's true. Besides, David was with me when you were in the can and getting caught," I lied.

"The whole time?" Scott asked.

"Well . . . most of the time."

He turned to David. "So did you do it?"

That was just like Scott — no beating around the bush.

I held my breath. I'd given David a way out. All he had to do was say that he didn't do it, that the guy who claimed to have overheard him was wrong.

David laughed. "It doesn't matter what I say. You think I did. So what are you going to do about it?" There was no mistaking either the tone of his voice or the fists clenched in his lap. It looked like David *wanted* to fight Scott.

Scott took a step toward David. "I'm going to —"

"Do nothing here!" I said, stepping in between them. "Are you two trying to cost me a place on the team?"

They both paused.

"You'll make this team, no problem," Scott said.

That was an encouraging thing to say.

"How can you miss when you see how pathetic the competition is?" Scott continued.

"They're not that bad," I said, gesturing to the players warming up around the gym.

"I wasn't talking about them. I was talking about him," Scott said, pointing at David. "Isn't everybody on the floor trying out for the team? Maybe I should have tried out, too."

"Maybe you should have," David snarled. "I hear they could use a team mascot. You could be the Homelands Hyena. After all, you gave a bunch of us a real good laugh . . . of course, people were laughing *at* you, not *with* you."

"Shut up!" Scott snapped. "You're lucky you're in that chair."

"Shows how stupid you are. The only one who's lucky I'm in this chair is you."

"Come on, guys, don't be stupid," I tried to reason. "You get into a fight and you'll both lose. You'll both be suspended." They grumbled, but slightly eased off.

"Besides, David is a pretty good ball player," I said.

"Him?" Scott laughed.

"Better than you by a long shot. I could take you," David said.

"You? What a laugh!"

"How about a game?" David asked.

"You have to be joking."

"The only joke is you," David snapped. "Want to play?"

"Any time, any place."

"How about right here and right now?" David countered.

"You can't," I said before Scott could say anything more. "The gym is reserved for people trying out for the team."

"Then I guess we can't —" Scott started to say.

David tucked his arms up like wings, flapped them, and made a clucking sound like a chicken. Once again, Scott looked like he was going to take a swing at him.

"Forget the basketball, let's just go out and settle this a different way," David suggested.

"Fine with me!" Scott agreed.

"Hold on!" I said, grabbing Scott by the arm. "Maybe if a couple of us guys who are trying out for the team played, too, then it would be all right."

"What do you mean?" Scott asked.

"A game of two-on-two. I'll take David on my side and you can choose anybody else you want to be on your team."

"Figures you'd pick David," Scott said.

"It doesn't mean anything. You can be on my side."

"Don't do me any favors. I'll take somebody else," Scott said angrily. "Although it would be easier to just step outside."

"We can do that, too," David snapped. "But first things first. Let's play ball . . . unless you're backing down?"

"I'm not backing down from anything," Scott said.

I looked up at the clock. "We only have about ten minutes until practice starts, so let's make it fast. But I think we have to have a side bet on the game."

"What did you have in mind?" Scott asked.

"How about if we win then everybody forgets about the roller rink."

"And if my team wins?" Scott asked.

"I'll buy you lunch for a week," David said.

"Make it two weeks and you have a deal," Scott said.

"We can make it three weeks if you like. It doesn't matter, because you aren't going to win," David said.

"Deal?" I asked.

Scott nodded. "Give me a minute to pick out my partner." He walked across the gym, looking at all the guys shooting hoops. He stopped and talked to a couple of players, who all pointed to the far side of the gym — at the guy who'd been giving me so much trouble under the net. His name was Greg. I'd been holding my own with him, but he was awfully strong. Scott flashed me a smile and then jogged over to Greg's side. Scott's back was to me as they started to talk. Greg looked shocked and then amused. He nodded in agreement and came back with Scott.

"I have myself a partner," Scott said.

"Let's set the rules. First team to ten baskets, cutthroat, so whoever scores gets to keep the ball. Any turnover and the ball has to clear the three-point line before the other team can score. Sound good?" David asked.

"Sounds like you can talk a good game," Scott chuckled.

"I can talk it and play it. That puts me two up on you."

"This should be a piece of cake," Greg said.

"If that's what you think, then you won't mind us getting first ball, will you?" David asked.

Scott shrugged and Greg nodded in agreement.

David wheeled out to the top of the key with the ball in his lap. "Check," he said as he threw the ball to Scott. Scott tossed it back. David caught it and before anybody could even react he launched the ball toward the net. It hit the rim and backboard and then dropped.

"That makes one," David announced as the three of us watched open-mouthed.

I retrieved the ball and threw it back out at him.

"That's your man. Cover him!" Greg yelled and Scott hurried out. Just before he got there, David put up another shot over his outstretched hands and it dropped too!

"Make that two up," David shouted.

I ran after the ball. I was just going to send it back to David when I stopped. Every single person in the gym — on the floor trying out for the team and sitting in the bleachers — was watching us. I swallowed hard and sent the ball back to him.

"I told you to cover him!" Greg bellowed.

Scott crowded out until he was standing right over top of David. David spun to one side and started dribbling, using his chair to shield the ball from Scott. I tried to take up a position in the low post. Greg pressed hard against my back, pushing and shoving and reaching a hand over my shoulder to try to deflect the pass we both knew was coming. David sent a crisp bounce pass that evaded Greg's outstretched hands, and I corralled it. I felt his hand shove into my back. I faked one way, went back the other, and put up the hook. It clanked off the rim and bounced off. Scott got the rebound and dribbled outside the three-point line.

"I've got him. You stay under the hoop!" David yelled out.

Scott sent up a wild shot that was a clear miss. As I went up for the rebound, I felt another push and Greg got the ball and put it back up for a basket.

"That makes one!" Scott called out.

* * *

"Time-out!" David yelled.

"What do you mean, 'time-out?'" Scott questioned.

"What don't you understand? I need a time-out to talk to my teammate."

"Forget it, just play the game!"

"Give it to them. They're not going to win anyway," Greg taunted. He really was a jerk.

David moved over to the side and I bent over beside him. I struggled to catch my breath. We were down nine baskets to seven.

"I can't believe we're losing to these guys," David said angrily.

"They're pretty good."

"They stink! We're just making them look good — actually, *you're* just making them look good. Do you want to win or don't you?"

"Of course, I want to win!"

"Then play like it! You're getting pushed around in the paint."

"I'm doing the best I can."

"No, you're not! Come on, Sean, something's wrong when I'm getting more vertical leap and pulling in more rebounds than you! Get mad. Don't let these jerks show us up! Okay?"

"Okay." He was right. I was being pushed around, and it was happening in front of everybody.

"I'm going to take the ball to the top of the key, feed it out to you, and you feed it back fast. I want you to break to my right, and I'll set a pick that'll separate you from Greg. If Scott switches off, you can beat him to the hoop."

I nodded and walked away to get ready for the feed.

"Check," David called as he bounced the ball to Scott, who instantly returned it. David set the play as he'd called it, and as I cut tightly around him, he spun to pick off my man. I brushed by and there was a clear path to the net. I heard a thunderous crash from behind as I laid the ball off the board and into the basket. I turned to see both Scott and Greg in a tangled mass on the floor.

"That wasn't fair!" Greg yelled as he got to his feet. "Moving pick, the basket doesn't count! It's our ball!"

"It was a fair pick!" David shouted. "If you can't stand a little physical play, why don't you try out for the school band instead?"

Scott had jumped up and there was a look of rage in his eyes. "You want physical play! I'll show you physical!"

I stepped over and planted myself so Scott would have to come straight through me. "The pick was fair," I said.

"How would you know?" Scott demanded. "Your back was to the play!"

"It was fair because my partner said it was," I answered without hesitating.

Greg brushed past Scott and crowded into my face. "I say it wasn't fair!"

"And I say it was," came a voice from over in the corner. All eyes turned. It was Coach.

"He was set. The pick was fair, the basket counts, and another word out of either of you two and it'll be a technical foul and a detention. Got it?" Coach asked.

Greg looked like he had more to say, but shut up. The clock right above Coach's head said four o'clock.

"I guess we should stop," I said apologetically.

"What's the score?" Coach asked.

"They're ahead, nine baskets to eight," I said.

Coach walked over and picked up the ball. He fired it out to David. "Finish what you started."

I walked out to David.

"Post up low. Hit the hook," he instructed.

As soon as I took position, Greg tried to push me farther out. I shifted a couple of times and he had trouble pinning me. David rifled a pass to me. I faked inside, then faded away with the hook shot. I watched over my shoulder as it dropped to tie the score. Kids started cheering and, as I turned to go back outside, I saw Coach clapping his hands along with them.

David started with the ball again. I took my position inside and Greg pushed against me with all his might. I looked up at David, who motioned for me to go to the other side. I pushed full force back against Greg, straining every muscle, and then, without warning, shifted to the side. He tumbled over onto his face. David fed me a sharp chest pass, I put up a short jumper that dropped and the game was over! David wheeled over and gave me a high five as people crowded around us and offered congratulations.

"Nice move," Coach said. "Very nice move. That's the sort of heads-up play I like to see — using your smarts as well as your size. Now let's get this practice started!"

Chapter 13

"My God, what happened to you?" I asked in amazement. David's face was bruised and cut up on one side.

"I cut myself shaving," he said with a laugh.

"No, come on, tell me what happened, really," I demanded. Had he and Scott got into it after they left the gym? Scott could be a goof, but he was a goof who kept his word . . . unless David provoked him. I could see that happening.

"I just had a little accident is all."

He started wheeling down the hall and I walked beside him. He hadn't been in school yesterday, the day after our little two-on-two game, and when I'd called last night I'd only got the answering machine. I just figured he had another doctor's appointment or was sick. I hadn't thought anything more about it until I saw his face.

"What sort of accident?" I asked, pressing him for more details.

"What are you, the police?" he demanded as he continued rolling down the hall.

"No, I just want to know."

"It was nothing . . . just a stupid accident. I fell down a couple of steps."

"You got banged up like that falling down a couple of steps?" I questioned.

"Actually there were three of them — four times."

"You fell down twelve steps!" I exclaimed.

"Sshhhh!" he hissed at me. "It's embarrassing enough without you broadcasting it to the whole school."

"Sorry," I apologized, lowering my voice. "How did it happen?"

"I was out at the mall. There were stairs. Six flights of three stairs with a long landing between each flight."

"And you didn't see them?" I asked.

"Oh, I saw them."

"If you saw them, how did you fall down them?"

"I thought I could get down them," he said, looking away.

"You thought what?" I demanded in astonishment.

He looked up at me and his eyes flashed with

anger. "I thought I could get down them is what I said. You've seen me get down three steps before. I do it all the time. I just figured it was the same thing."

"That's crazy! Why didn't you just take the elevator? There must be elevators in the mall."

"I didn't *want* to take the elevator. I almost made it. I got down the first two flights with no problem. Actually, I got down all the stairs . . . it's just that I wasn't in the chair for the last four flights. It was harder on the chair then it was on me."

"The chair looks okay. Wait a second, this isn't your chair."

"It's my old chair. One of the wheels is sort of bent on my regular one, and it's getting fixed. It's no big deal. It's just a chair, nobody died."

"But you could have!"

"But I didn't. Stuff happens."

"Only to you," I said.

"Now you sound like my parents."

"Well, at least it was stairs," I said softly. I was glad it didn't have anything to do with Scott.

"What do you mean?" David asked.

"You know . . . I was just thinking that may- be . . . you know, you look like somebody beat you up."

"Yeah, and who do you think would do that?" David demanded.

I knew from his tone and posture that I should

change the subject, but I couldn't figure out how. "I just thought that maybe . . . you know . . . that after the game the other day that Scott and you might have . . . taken it outside."

"We did take it outside."

"You fought?"

"Nope, came close but we didn't." He paused. "At least not that day."

"What do you mean?"

"I don't like the guy and he doesn't like me. Just a matter of time till we come to blows." David's expression changed. "You thought he beat me up, didn't you?"

I nodded.

"First off, he couldn't, but if he had, so what?"

"So . . . you know . . . it wouldn't have been right," I stammered, feeling increasingly uncomfortable.

"Not right because you figure I could take him, or not right because I'm in a chair?" David demanded harshly.

I didn't know what to say. I just knew he was getting angrier looking by the second.

David continued. "And if I told you he had beaten me up, were you planning on doing something about it?"

"Well . . ."

"Because if you were, you'd better not! I don't need you to fight my battles. I can take care of myself without you sticking your nose in!

Understand?"

"I just want to help."

"Is that what you've been doing the last few days? Following me around and asking me where I was going all the time? Were you trying to protect me from Scott?"

I didn't answer.

"You want to do something to help me? Leave me alone!" he screamed as he started wheeling away.

I took a few steps after him but stopped. There was no point in chasing him.

* * *

I sat silently beside David through homeroom, and then we went off in different directions for our next two classes. I got a little worried when he didn't show for math. No matter how angry he was with me, that was no reason to skip class. I grabbed my lunch from my locker. On my way to the cafeteria, I got caught up in a conversation with a couple of guys trying out for the team. They had some good things to say about the two-on-two game — Greg wasn't the most popular person and they'd enjoyed us beating him. I excused myself and hurried off. Moving across the cafeteria, I saw the girls sitting at our usual table but didn't see David anywhere. He was usually late, but not this late. I sat down beside Caroline and we all exchanged hellos.

"Where's David?" Lisa asked.

"I don't know. He wasn't in our last class," I answered. "But I'm not sure if he wants to eat lunch with me, anyway."

"Is he mad at you, too?" Lisa asked.

"Who else is he mad at?" I asked.

"Me."

"Why?"

"I don't know, but I must have said —"

"You didn't say anything wrong!" Christina interrupted. "Sometimes he just acts like a jerk!"

"Come on, don't be hard on him," Lisa pleaded.

"I'm not. I just don't like to see my friends being treated badly," Christina said.

"He doesn't treat me bad . . . not all the time," Lisa said softly and everybody fell into silence. She looked like she was close to tears. "Excuse me," she said and hurried away from the table.

"I'll go after her," Christina said and followed after Lisa.

"Why doesn't Christina like David?" I asked.

"She likes him," Caroline answered. "We all like him. It's just that he can be so . . . he just says such nasty things sometimes . . . you know what I mean, right?"

I nodded. Of course, I knew what she meant.

"And it's been getting worse lately. Lisa's only trying to be friendly, and he said the most awful things to her the other day." She paused. "Maybe you could talk to him."

I laughed. "I was hoping Lisa could talk to him for *me*."

"This morning we saw him at the end of the hall and we waved and called and he just turned around and took off. I know he saw us," Caroline said.

"Maybe he didn't want you to see his face," I said, thinking it through as I was talking.

"What do you mean?"

"It's all banged up. He fell down some steps. Maybe he didn't want Lisa to see him like that," I offered.

"Maybe. But that doesn't excuse the other times. I don't think Lisa would let anybody else treat her badly. I think she takes it because she feels sorry for him or something."

Alarm bells went off in my head. "Has she said she feels sorry for him?"

"Not in so many words. I can just tell . . . you know, by the way she talks to him."

And I knew if Caroline could tell, then David could tell, too. Nothing would bother him more than somebody feeling sorry for him.

"I better go," I said, standing up.

"Aren't you hungry?" Christina asked.

"No, not anymore. I'm going to go look for David."

* * *

I searched for him for the rest of the lunch period without any success. Finally, in desperation, with the bell about to ring, I went to the office and asked. It was a risk. If he was just skipping classes, then I could get him in big trouble. The secretary told me that she wasn't supposed to give out information about another student, but since I was his host — how did she know I was his host? — it would be all right. She said that David had come to the office because he was feeling dizzy and sick to his stomach and that his father came and got him. At least I knew where he was and that he was all right, but it didn't give me a chance to talk to him.

All through my afternoon classes I thought about what had happened. I still didn't think I'd done anything that was really that bad. Friends take care of friends. It didn't matter if David was in a chair or not. If somebody beat up a friend of mine, they'd better know I was coming after them. That's what I did last year with Scott — I kept on stepping into troubles he'd created. Of course, none of that helped me figure out what I was going to say to David, though.

After last period French, I quickly pulled on my shoes and tied my laces. Coach was a fanatic about people being late. I'd had to stay a few minutes after class because I'd said something to the teacher she didn't like. She told me how "surprised" she was by my outburst because I'd been doing so well. I was even more surprised than she was. The words had just jumped out of my mouth.

I grabbed my shirt, slammed the locker, which echoed off the empty walls of the change room, and hurried out to the gym.

"McGregor!" Coach yelled and motioned for me to come to him.

I was in for it now. The big clock behind his head showed it was one minute after four.

"You showed some nice stuff the other day in that two-on-two game."

"Thanks," I mumbled. I didn't know what I was more thrilled about, the compliment or the fact that it looked like I wasn't going to be chewed out.

"I'd been waiting for you to show more under the hoop." He slapped me on the back. "I was wondering, who was calling the plays for your team?"

"Mostly my friend, David," I reluctantly admitted. "But I ran a couple of them."

"He's a smart player, and it looks like he pushed you into playing a little smarter, too."

"I guess so."

"Get yourself one of the yellow jerseys. I want you to start this practice on line one. Just keep doing what you were doing during that two-on-two game."

"Sure!" I said enthusiastically as I rushed over to get the jersey.

"McGregor!" he called out.

I stopped and turned. "Yeah?"

"Is your friend coming to watch today?"

I shook my head.

"Too bad. Tell him he's welcome any time."

"I will," I said. Now I knew what I could say to David.

Chapter 14

I didn't even bother to shower after the practice, I just hurried out of the school. I was still feeling high. I'd played better than I ever had before and I knew that confidence builds confidence. I was due home soon, and Mom would worry if I was too late, but I wanted to talk to David. I didn't want to do it tomorrow, when people would be buzzing all around us, or by telephone, which he could just refuse to answer or simply hang up on me. I needed to do it face to face. I wanted to explain, and maybe even apologize, though I still figured I hadn't done anything wrong. Telling him what Coach had said would just give me an excuse to start up a conversation. Once we started talking, there was no telling where things would go. I was nervous to bring up anything about Lisa, but I knew Caroline would like it if I at least mentioned it.

I sprinted off the school grounds and then kept on running, past my street, until I came to Chambers. I slowed down to a walk. I wanted to catch my breath before I got there. I stopped in front of number 170. A couple of times David had mentioned inviting me to his house, but the invitation never came.

Strange, there was a full set of stairs leading up to the front door. That couldn't be right. I was expecting a ramp. Had I remembered the number wrong? I peered down the driveway and caught a glimpse of a wooden ramp at the back. This had to be the right place.

I started up the driveway. There was no car and the garage was open and empty. Maybe nobody was home. This thought gave me a little more confidence. I circled around to the back and started up the ramp. I was surprised by how steep it was. Stopping in front of the door, I could hear loud music. Obviously somebody was home, unless they left it on when they weren't there as a trick to fool burglars.

I had just taken a deep breath and had raised my hand to knock when the door opened unexpectedly. A woman appeared in the doorway, holding a plastic bag and singing along loudly to the music. She practically bumped into me, shrieked, tossed the bag high into the air, and jumped backward. I leaped back, too, as the bag hit the porch and garbage splattered everywhere.

"Oh, my goodness, you scared me!" she exclaimed.

"I-I'm sorry," I stammered. "I was just going to knock when you opened the door."

"It's not your fault. I was just lost in the music, that's all."

"I wanted to speak to David."

"He's not home. Say, are you Sean?"

I nodded.

"Please, please come in! I'm David's mother."

She was tall and thin and had lots of blonde hair all piled up on top of her head. She really didn't look like a mother.

I stepped around the garbage splattered on the porch as she ushered me into the house. Entering, I was assaulted by the booming throb of the music.

"Let me turn that down!" she yelled out over the music and hurried into the other room. She reappeared. "There, that's better. David has told us all about you!"

I wasn't sure if I liked that or not. "Is David okay? When he didn't show for lunch I went to the office and they told me he went home early."

"He was complaining about his head hurting and he threw up. We were told to watch for those things in case he suffered a concussion in the fall. His dad took him to see the doctor."

"I hope he's all right."

"I'm sure he will be. You get good at what you have practice doing, and David has had lots of practice falling down. He's as tough as nails," she said, and I nodded in agreement. "Do you want to sit down and wait? I'm sure they won't be much longer."

"No, I better get going." I was already late. "I just wanted to tell him about basketball."

"Does he talk to you about basketball?" she asked. She looked startled.

"Yeah. All the time."

"He doesn't talk about it to us at all . . . not since the accident."

"He really knows the game, and boy does he ever have a great shot!" I said.

"You've seen him shoot?" She sounded even more surprised.

"We've played twenty-one a couple of times, and we had a really good game of two-on-two the other day and —"

"And he was playing?" she interrupted. Her expression and tone of voice had changed from surprise to shock.

Had I done something bad? Maybe he wasn't supposed to do things like that because of his condition.

"I-I'm sorry," I stammered again. "I didn't mean to do anything wrong."

"No, no, you don't understand! You didn't do

anything wrong. Honestly. I'm just surprised, pleasantly surprised, to hear that he was playing. They told us that would be a good sign."

"They?"

"The . . . the people at the hospital." Now she suddenly looked away, like she'd said something she shouldn't have.

"David was such a talented player. Such a wonderful basketball player." She paused. "Come, let me show you."

I followed her out of the kitchen and down a hallway. She pushed open a door. From the unmade bed, the dirty clothes balled up on the floor, and the posters on the walls I figured this had to be David's room. One whole wall was dominated by an almost life-sized picture of a basketball player. It wasn't like a store bought poster, but a painting.

His mother saw me staring. "Nice painting, isn't it?"

I nodded. "Did David do it?"

"Yes, he did. He is quite a talented artist. Wait a minute, how did you even know to ask? Did he tell you he liked to paint?"

I shook my head. "He didn't mention painting at all."

Her face, which had looked hopeful, suddenly deflated in disappointment.

"I just thought he might paint because he draws so well," I said.

Her face lit up again. "You've seen his drawings?"

"Yes, and, of course, he did the illustrations when we did a project together."

"That's wonderful!" She reached over, and, to my complete shock, gave me a hug.

"Yeah, I guess it is," I muttered, struggling for words, embarrassed by this show of emotion.

She released her hold.

"It is! You see, David has always been very artistic, very talented. He always wanted to be either a professional basketball player or an artist. But he hasn't picked up a brush since the accident, and, as far as we knew, hadn't drawn either." She stared at the painting with a far-away look. The silence was making me uncomfortable.

"Um . . . you wanted to show me something."

"Oh, of course," she said.

She opened up the closet door and pulled a cardboard box down from a shelf.

"I wanted you to see this," she said. She put the box on the floor and took a big book out of it. "This is David's," she said, handing it to me. "Have a look."

I opened the cover. Inside was a newspaper article topped by a large color picture of a group of boys holding up a trophy.

"That's when David's team won the regional championship," she said.

I looked harder at the picture. There was

David, front and center, with his hand holding the trophy aloft. He looked a lot the same, only there was no chair.

"He was the captain of the team, won the scoring championship, and was the league MVP."

"He must have been good," I mumbled.

"So good that he was already starting to attract interest from university and college scouts. Isn't that something, to be scouted by those people before he even got to high school?"

"That's like a dream." My father's dream.

"Turn the page. You'll see picture after picture. He won almost every place he ever played. And you know the best thing?" she continued. "Despite it all, he never let his head get swollen. He was just about the easiest-going, happiest kid I ever met, just a delight to be around and so much fun and . . ." she paused and looked sad. "I guess that the accident took away more than his legs."

I felt a knot grow in my stomach and I had to look away. My eyes fell on the cardboard box. I could see that it was filled with trophies.

"He sure won a lot of trophies," I said.

"I'd almost lost count of how many," she replied.

I'd won a few myself, not nearly as many as David, but a few. I had a special shelf in my room to put them on. But why weren't David's on display instead of in a box tucked away in his closet?

"It's a shame about the trophies," his mother said.

I didn't understand what she meant and just looked at her. She picked up one of the bigger trophies and handed it to me.

I instantly recognized it as being the city championship trophy I'd seen in the picture on the first page of the album. There was one difference from the picture, though: the top was broken off. I looked back into the box. All the trophies were disfigured or smashed or damaged. How could this have happened?

"David did it," she said, answering my unspoken question. "It was after the accident, while he was in the rehabilitation center. The social workers told us to bring things to his room, things that were important to him. We knew how much the trophies meant to him, how much basketball meant to him. We had no idea he'd do this. It wasn't until he moved back home that we found everything smashed.

"When we saw what he had done, we called the center and spoke to his social worker. She said he was angry about not being able to do what he loved doing. She wanted to start seeing him again, but David refused."

I picked up one of the other trophies. On top were the jagged, broken legs of a basketball player. On the front was a plate: "Playoff Most Valuable Player."

"That one was special. I remember being there when he won it. I was there when he won most of them. I guess when you have only one child, you spend a lot of time with him."

I looked at the trophy again. There was a date listed on the plate; it was last year's date! I couldn't believe that the accident had only happened in the past year. Somehow I'd thought it was years and years ago. Last year while I was doing nothing but getting into trouble David was a basketball star . . . walking and running . . . and not in a chair. It was too much for me to even think about it.

"What are you doing?"

Startled, I turned around to see David in the doorway. Quickly I lowered the broken trophy into the box. I felt like I'd been caught stealing.

"You have no right to be looking in there!" he said loudly.

"David, he was just —"

"I'm not just talking to him!" David interrupted. "Both of you get out of my room! Now!" he screamed as he rolled past us into the far corner.

His mother took me by the arm. "Come on," she said quietly and led me away.

I felt like my feet were made of cement and my mouth was filled with cotton. I could barely move, and even if I'd thought of something to say, I wouldn't have been able to force the words out.

David's mother stopped at the door and turned back toward him. "If there's anything you want . . ."

"I want to be left alone!" he screamed. "Close the door and leave me alone!"

To my utter shock he reached over, grabbed a book off his dresser, and hurled it at us. I ducked as the book flew through the air with the pages pinwheeling and smashed against the wall. Without saying a word, his mother quietly closed the door behind us. "I'm sorry you had to be part of that. Sometimes he just gets that way, all angry and bitter. I guess I can't blame him," she said.

I'd seen him mad before. A couple of those times were at me, but I'd never seen him with such a look of total rage. I almost expected him to get up out of the chair and come over and take a swing at us.

"The only good part is it passes as quickly as it comes. If you want to wait a half hour or so, he'll be okay," she said.

"I can't wait . . . I better get going," I said hastily. "I have to get home."

"After he cools down, I'll explain to him that you couldn't stay."

I nodded dumbly and followed her into the kitchen. Just then, the door opened and a large, bearded man ducked under the door frame and came in. I took a step backward. He was one of the biggest people I'd ever seen in my life. I prayed this was David's father.

"Honey, this is Sean."

"David's friend?" he questioned in a deep

rumbling voice.

I nodded. He came forward and reached out his hand. I did the same and my hand disappeared in his huge mitt. "I'm really happy to meet you. My name is Joe, but everybody calls me Tiny," he boomed.

"Tiny?" I questioned.

He laughed. "Yeah, it's kind of a joke."

"What did the doctor say about David?" his mother asked, obviously concerned.

"Didn't David tell you?" Tiny asked.

She shook her head.

"He has a concussion, but he's okay."

"Thank the Lord!" she exclaimed.

"Say," Tiny said, "since you're here and it's almost dinnertime, do you want to join us?"

"Um . . . no . . . I have to get going."

"Well, it's good to meet you. Come back again for dinner some time soon." He reached out again and shook my hand. "Say, where is David?"

"In his room. He had a meltdown," David's mother explained.

Tiny nodded knowingly. "Bad?"

"I've seen worse."

"It has been a while since his last one," Tiny said. "Maybe it's better you can't stay, after all. Do you need a ride home?"

"No, it's okay. I just live a few blocks away. But, thanks anyway."

"No, no," he said. "You don't have to thank us.

We owe you the thanks — for being there for David, for being his friend."

"I better get going," I mumbled and hurried out the door. I wasn't sure how good a friend I was. Or how good a friend David would let anybody become.

Chapter 15

"Sean, get going or you're going to be late!" my mother yelled down the hall.

I quickly grabbed my backpack. I didn't want to be late. Late meant detentions, and detentions meant not being able to get to basketball.

I'd had trouble getting to sleep last night. Whenever I'd closed my eyes, I could see the mutilated trophies, or worse, that look of pure fury on David's face when he came into the room. Finally, exhausted, I'd dropped off to sleep, but overslept the alarm.

I raced down the hall. Mom was standing with my lunch in one hand and the open front door in the other.

"I'll see you after practice," I said.

"Practice? I thought it was still tryouts?" she asked.

"Well . . . I guess it is . . . it's just I figure I've made it."

She just smiled, but she had that look that said, "don't count your chickens until they're hatched."

"I better get going."

"You better." She reached over and gave me a hug.

I closed the door, leaped down the porch stairs, and ran down the driveway. Then I skidded to a stop. David was sitting on the sidewalk at the end of the driveway.

"I was wondering when you were coming out," he said.

"I slept in," I managed to say. Why was he here? It wasn't like we walked to school together. He didn't want to do something stupid like fight me . . . did he?

He looked at his watch. "The bell's going to go in fifteen minutes. Can we still get there on time?"

"We can if we run."

"Run? How about if we roll really fast?"

"Yeah, of course . . . I'm sorry . . . I meant I have to run."

"Actually you don't. If you're with me you've got all the time you need. Don't you remember that first day we met?"

"Hard to forget . . . I still have a sore spot on one rib."

David laughed. "I didn't mean that part. I meant when we went to that first class. We were late."

"Oh, yeah, I was positive I was going to make my second trip to the office in less than twenty minutes."

"But you didn't, right? Because you were with me. It's really hard to get into trouble when you're with me. I never get sent to the office for being late. I'll tell them you had to help me and that's why you were late, too. Instead of being in trouble, you'll be treated like you're a hero or something. You know, like a boy scout helping a little old lady across the street."

"Are you sure?"

"Trust me," he said, flashing me a big smile. It was reassuring to see him smile, and I couldn't help but return it. "But just to be sure, we better not be too late." He turned and started rolling, and I trotted along side.

The side of his face still looked pretty ugly. If anything, the bruising was even worse than yesterday. I remembered last year when I'd "caught" a deflected puck with my eye. It got uglier and uglier for three days.

"My father already invited you for a meal. He said I'm supposed to make sure you come for dinner."

"Yeah . . . sure . . . when?" I asked.

"He wants you to come next Thursday. Thursdays are special."

"What's so special about them?"

"My father gets off work early, so he always cooks dinner that night."

"Your father cooks?"

"He really enjoys tinkering in the kitchen."

Tiny just didn't strike me as the sort of guy who "tinkered."

"His meals are always good, but sometimes they're a bit offbeat. So, can I tell him you'll be there?"

"I was planning on spending that Thursday finishing up that biography project we have for social science. It's due on Friday."

"You really don't believe in getting things done early, do you?"

"I do my best work at the last minute, but I guess I can work on it Wednesday night. Have you finished?" I asked.

"No," David admitted.

"It's hard writing about yourself."

"It's not that. I've had trouble getting pictures. A lot of our stuff is still in storage."

"Maybe you could draw the pictures. You're such a good artist."

"I never draw myself. Never." His voice was hard and cold for a second, then went back to normal. "So are you coming for dinner?"

"I guess . . . if you want me to."

"Why wouldn't I?" he asked.

I didn't answer. There was no point in saying

what we both already knew.

"I was mad, so what?" David said.

"I didn't mean to be snooping. It all just sort of happened," I explained. "I'm sorry."

David snorted. "My mother told me to say one more thing. I have to tell you I'm sorry for yelling at you. Sometimes I can be a jerk."

"Thanks for the apology," I said. "And you're right, sometimes you can be a jerk." I took a deep breath and decided to continue. "And not just with me."

"What do you mean?" David asked, and I could hear that change in his tone of voice again.

"Lisa."

"What about her?"

"Sometimes you don't treat her very well."

"What are you, her mother?"

"No, I'm her friend . . . and your friend as well."

David didn't answer, but I thought he picked up his speed slightly.

"She likes you," I said. "I think she'd like to go out with you."

"Yeah, right," he snapped.

"She does, I know!"

"There's a big difference between wanting to date somebody and feeling sorry for them," David said.

I wanted to say something but I figured it might be both; she did like him, but she felt sorry for him, as well. It was hard not to sometimes.

David looked like he was fighting back tears.

"It must be hard," I said quietly.

"I get by."

"I understand."

David stopped and spun around so suddenly that he almost knocked me over. "No, you don't."

"I guess I don't," I admitted, "but I'd like to try."

"Would you really?" David asked.

I nodded.

He stared at me — hard. "Are you doing anything tomorrow?"

"Just some chores. I have to cut the grass."

"And after that?"

"I'm free for the day," I said.

"Good. Right after you finish the grass, come on over. How early can you be there?"

"Maybe around nine. What did you have in mind?" I said a bit anxiously.

"If I told you, it would ruin the surprise. Just come as early as you can, and tell your parents you won't be home until around supper."

Chapter 16

I knocked on the front door again — this time much louder. There was still no answer. I peeked through the glass and around the little curtains covering the window, but I couldn't see anything except a little sliver of the living room.

I'd rushed through my chores and run all the way over to David's to be early and now he wasn't even here. Part of me was strangely relieved. I'd been trying to think what he might have in mind for me and was more than a little nervous.

I walked along the length of the porch and peered down the side of the house. There weren't any cars in the drive and the garage door was wide open. A hint of movement in the garage caught my eye, and, using my hand to shield my eyes from the bright sunlight, I stared into the darkness. It was David. I leaped over the railing and landed on the drive.

"How you doing?" I yelled as I trotted down the side of the house toward him.

"Not bad. You ready?" David asked.

"Yeah, I guess so," I answered, although I wanted to ask "ready for what?"

"Good, have a seat."

"But I don't want to sit down."

"You have to . . . there." David pointed to a second wheelchair.

"You want me to sit in that?"

"Yeah, that's the idea. You're going to spend some time in a chair — that's what we're going to do today."

I slowly walked over to the chair. I hesitated before starting to lower myself into it.

"Before you sit down though, I better warn you," David said.

I straightened up. "Warn me about what?"

"Sitting in a wheelchair is supposed to mean bad luck."

"Yeah, sure." I laughed nervously.

"I'm not kidding. I've never met anybody who was in a wheelchair who hadn't suffered from the worst luck in the world."

Embarrassed, I looked away from him and at the chair. I recognized it immediately from the automobile and rock stickers on the side — it was David's good chair. David was in his spare chair.

He didn't like that chair nearly as much as the one he usually used. I remembered how much he'd complained when his good chair needed to be repaired. He said it wasn't padded as well and the ride wasn't as smooth.

I turned around and started to lower myself into the chair. As I did, it skittered away and I almost missed it completely, landing on the very edge of the seat.

"That's your first lesson," David said as he rolled over to my side. "These things on the side are the brakes. Never try to get in or out of the chair without making sure they're locked. Understand?"

"Yeah, I guess so."

"Good. Here's how you work them." He leaned across me and clicked two small metal latches, one on each wheel, so they dug into the rubber tires. "When they're locked the chair isn't going any-where." He then clicked them off. "Now you try it."

I reached down and locked and unlocked the brakes a couple of times.

"Now that you know how to stop, let's give you some lessons on how to go. First, take the foot rests, swing them into place, and lift up your feet."

I lifted my right foot to push one of the rests into place.

"No, not like that!" David practically yelled. "If this experiment is going to work, you have to pretend your legs don't! Reach down with your hands and push it into place. Then use both hands to lift your leg up onto the rest. I don't want you to use the muscles of your legs to help you at all. Just pretend your legs are dead weight."

I started to laugh, but then I saw that he was completely serious. I did as he asked. It felt strange.

"So far so good. Do you know how to make the chair go?"

"I think I have an idea," I replied sarcastically. I reached down and took hold of the metal inner ring of the wheels and gave myself a big pull forward and sailed across the room.

"Not bad, huh?" I asked.

"Real impressive. There were a couple of things I was going to say to you, but you're just such an expert I'll save my breath."

I started back across the floor toward him.

"Ooooch!" I screamed as the fingers of my left hand jammed in the spokes of the wheel and the chair skidded to a stop. I removed my hand and examined it carefully, flexing the fingers. They were throbbing but there were no cuts.

"You have to watch your fingers in the spokes," David said. "That was one of the things I wanted to explain to you, even though you're such an expert you hardly need my help," he said, sarcasm dripping off each word.

"Okay, okay, I get the idea," I said.

"You sure? I was just hoping that somebody as expert as you could explain things to me."

I held up my hands. "I give up."

David smiled. "People have a tendency, especially at first, to keep their hands and wrists too close in. This causes trouble. Your fingers can get caught in the spokes, and your wrists end up rubbing against the wheels. It hurts a little when you're only moving slow, like you were. But if you're really moving and it happens, then you're in big trouble. Not only does your finger almost get sliced off, but you can get thrown right out of the chair."

"It's happened to you?" I asked.

"Yeah . . . once . . . only once." He smiled. "Of course, that isn't the most dangerous thing that can happen."

"What do you mean?" I asked apprehensively.

"Like I said, you have to keep your wrists wide. If you don't, then the sleeves of your shirt drag along the wheel. They get really dirty and worn."

"Yeah? I don't see the danger."

"The danger is my mother. She told me she'd kill me if I wore out any more shirts."

"I'll watch out," I answered, feeling relieved that was all he meant. I angled my wrists away from the chair and wheeled across the floor and did another tight turn to come back to David's side.

"I'll be careful . . . very careful."

"I bet you will. Come on, I want to see you go up and down the driveway a few times." David rolled out of the garage and onto the drive.

I felt a little self-conscious. It was different fooling around in the chair here in the garage where nobody could really see me than rolling along the driveway where anybody could pass by.

"Come on!" David yelled.

There was no way out of this. The garage was slightly higher than the driveway, and I rolled down a little ramp of asphalt. The chair rocked slightly to one side.

"Try to take bumps straight on, not one wheel and then the other. You can get away with it on a small drop like that, but if it's any bigger, the chair will tip over."

"When I walked in I didn't even realize there was a bump," I said.

"You wouldn't have. Lots of things you don't notice walking will come up and hit you in the face when you're in a chair. You'll find out, but first things first. Let's see you go down the driveway."

I started toward the street. I moved unsteadily, wobbling from side to side.

"Pump both wheels at the same time!" David called out.

I followed his directions. Things did seem to settle down, and I even started to pick up a little bit of speed. I hadn't realized it, but there was a slight slope to the driveway. I grabbed hold of the rings and brought the chair to a halt just before the sidewalk. I looked up and down the street.

Thank goodness nobody was watching. I firmly gripped the rings and pushed forward with my right hand while I pulled back with the left, which spun me around to face David.

"Very impressive!" he yelled, clapping his hands. "Maybe you did learn a few things from watching me!"

I started back up the drive. The slight incline made the trip back much harder. It was amazing how the almost imperceptible slope registered in the muscles of my arms.

I pulled up beside David. "What now? I think I have the driveway pretty well mastered."

"Well, in that case, I figured we'd go to the mall . . . if that's okay with you."

"The mall? Sure. My mom's birthday is coming up, and I have to get something for her." I started to get up from the chair, but David reached over and placed a hand on my shoulder, holding me in place.

"What are you doing?" David asked.

"Getting up . . . aren't we going to the mall?"

"Yes, we are. Me in my chair," he paused, "and you in yours."

Chapter 17

"The mall is a long way off."

"I've gone there by myself before," David said.

"You went all that way?"

"It's not that far. I can make it in less than twenty minutes," David said. "Of course, I know what I'm doing. With you rolling along behind me, it'll probably take longer."

"I don't know," I offered hesitantly. Playing around in the chair in his driveway was one thing, but going to the mall . . . being in public like that.

"Look, you said you wanted to understand what it's like to be in a chair."

"Yeah, I do, but —"

"But nothing! You figure a trip up and down the driveway can help you to understand how I have to live?"

"No, I don't, it's just . . ."

"Look, I'm going to the mall. Either you get up, park the chair in the garage, and go home, or you come with me. What's it going to be?"

Even though he'd given me a choice, he really hadn't. "Let's go."

He nodded. "Good. You'd better put these on." He pulled a pair of gloves out of the side of his chair and tossed them into my lap. I picked them up. They were almost like the gloves my mother used when she gardened.

"Why do I need these?"

"They'll protect your hands from getting all worn, you know, rubbing off the skin and getting cuts and blisters," David explained.

"But I've never seen you wear gloves."

David pumped once and his chair slid right up beside mine. He held out his hands. "Feel."

I gave him a questioning look.

"I said 'feel them,' not 'hold them.'" He reached out and took one of my hands. "Compare my hands to yours."

His hands were hard and rough and covered with calluses.

"I don't need gloves anymore because my hands have toughened up. But if you don't wear them, by the end of today your hands will look like two puffy pieces of raw meat."

That didn't sound good.

"Think about basketball. Your sense of touch

would be way off if that happened, and you don't have the greatest outside shot at the best of times."

I didn't need any more convincing. I quickly pulled on the gloves.

David started down the sidewalk and I followed after him. I wanted to catch up to him, but there wasn't space on the sidewalk for the two of us to be side by side. The gap between us quickly grew, despite my best efforts to move closer. I pushed on harder, and the rhythmic "bump, bump" of the wheels against the sidewalk squares quickened. A couple of times I was jarred as the wheels either dropped off, or bounced, onto a square that was a different elevation. It was funny how the sidewalk seemed level enough to the eye, but I could feel the changes in the seat of my pants.

"You're not doing bad . . . for a beginner," David said. He was sitting at the edge of the road, waiting for me. "How are your arms feeling?"

"Fine," I lied. I could already feel some strain in my upper arms. "I'm more worried about my bum. Why don't these things have better suspension?"

"This is nothing. Sometimes it can be so rough it feels like my fillings could rattle out of my teeth." He paused. "We have a choice now. We can cross the road right here or go to the end of the block," he said, motioning to the traffic lights at the corner.

We still had a long way to go and I didn't want

to add any more distance than I had to. But I knew crossing the street could be scary. "Let's go," I said quickly before I could change my mind.

David immediately bumped down the curb and onto the road. I went to follow, but remembered about both wheels going down together and straightened them out. I braced myself, lifting my bottom slightly off the seat as I went down off the curb. I wasn't sure if maybe that was cheating a little bit. Anyway, despite my efforts, the drop was still jarring.

"Hurry up!" David yelled. He was waiting at just my side of the center line. "That truck will only get bigger!"

I looked down the road. A large truck was coming my way. Fast! I hesitated for a second, fighting the urge to jump out of the chair and get back to the safety of the sidewalk.

"Come on! As long as you come now you still have plenty of time!" David called out.

I pumped my arms and shot across the two lanes.

"Whoa!" David yelled, holding out an arm to stop me. "No good running from the truck, just to get hit by a car."

No sooner had the words left his mouth when a car zipped past us, going the other way. Involuntarily, I pushed myself against the back of the chair and away from the car. A split second later, the truck roared by.

"As soon as the next car passes, we'll go. I'm going to jump the curb, but you better aim for that ramp over there," he said, pointing to a driveway. "Remember, try to take it straight on. Just as you get to the ramp, lean back in the chair and give yourself a big push. That'll jump your front wheels off the ground a little so you can get up. Understand?"

"Yeah, I guess," I mumbled, although my attention had been diverted by a couple of cars racing by.

"Now!" David said.

I didn't even bother looking, just headed off, trusting that David knew it was safe. He went straight ahead and I aimed off toward the driveway. In the distance I saw the light change to green. I pumped hard. A rush of fear came over me, and I had to fight the urge to head straight to the curb and ride along the side. I needed to be out enough to hit the ramp on an angle. I came to the ramp, grabbed the left wheel to spin me to the left, and then with a mighty heave pumped both wheels, and jumped up the ramp and onto the sidewalk. I took a deep breath. Sweat was rolling down my arms, and I realized that I was shaking.

"What did you think of that?" David asked.

"Not much," I answered truthfully. "Everything looked so huge!"

"You've never seen traffic from a chair before. Everything is different." David paused. "Everything."

* * *

In the distance I could see the mall. I had never been so glad to see something in my life.

"Be extra careful as we cross the parking lot. Cars are looking for other vehicles and people walking. We're too low to be seen in the rearview mirrors of trucks and vans and even minivans."

Maybe because of David's warning, the crossing was uneventful and we reached the walkway surrounding the mall. Cars were parked along the curb and people were standing all around the front doors. A lot of them seemed to be watching us. I tried to ignore them and focused only on the entrance, which, fortunately, was easy because of the automatic doors. I rolled in after David.

The mall looked busy. People were rushing and pushing and moving all around us. I felt like a rock in the middle of a fast-moving stream as they funneled around us. I was also shocked by how small I felt. Everybody, even little kids, towered over my head and blocked me in.

I hoped I didn't run into anyone I knew. What if Scott or the guys or Caroline were here! I'd have to think up some explanation.

"Where do you want to go?" David asked.

"I don't know."

"I thought you wanted to pick up something."

"Oh, yeah, a birthday present for my mother," I said. "I was going to get her some sort of gadget for the kitchen. She loves cooking . . . like your father."

"And you love eating. Sounds like a match made in heaven," David laughed. "Where's the store?"

"It's this way," I said as I started off in that direction.

"Is it on this floor?" David called out.

I turned around. "Um . . . second floor."

"Then we need an elevator, and the elevators are in the other direction. I'll show you."

Once again I followed after David. I didn't really mind, though. It was like being behind a snowplow: he broke a trail through the legs and strollers that filled the mall. And that was mainly what I saw from my vantage point in the chair — legs and strollers. The heads of almost everybody were above my eye level. And when I did look up, I saw that people were staring at me and David. But as soon as I caught their eye, they quickly turned away.

David stopped in front of the elevator. I'd been to this mall dozens and dozens of times, but I'd never used the elevators before. No sooner had I got to David's side when the doors opened, and a wave of mothers pushing strollers washed out of the elevator. I tried to shift to the side to let them pass, but I wasn't quick enough and they had to maneuver around us.

"Do you boys need any help?" one of the mothers asked. She had one hand on the elevator door, keeping it open, and the other on her stroller.

"What?" I asked.

"Do you need any help?" she repeated, this time louder and slower.

"We're okay," David answered.

The woman took her hand off the elevator door and, as David and I rolled by, she reached out and patted me on the shoulder. Her action caught me off guard and before I could react, the door slid shut and we started to move.

David chuckled to himself as the elevator "binged" and the door slid open to the second floor. I was still facing toward the back of the elevator and I tried to spin myself around. In my rush, I pulled the wrong wheel and banged into the wall and then David. I tried to turn the other way.

"Here, let me help you," a woman's voice sang out, and I felt myself being pulled backward. The wheels bumped off the elevator and past a convoy of strollers. David rolled off by himself.

"There you go, dear," the woman said and got on the elevator. It quickly filled and the door closed. David and I were alone.

"Welcome to my world," David said.

"That was bizarre. That woman grabbed me and dragged me out like I was —"

"In a stroller?" David asked, interrupting me.

Instantly I thought back to the time I'd done that with David and how angry he'd gotten. "Yeah. And what about that lady on the first floor?

She reached out and patted me on the shoulder!" I said in disbelief.

"It could have been worse. It could have been on the top of your head."

"Yeah, right," I answered.

"Today's going to be a big shock for you. Being in a chair makes you public property, and everybody thinks they can do their good deed for the day with you. You never did that," he hastily reassured me. "And you never talked to me like I was an idiot. Not even the first time."

That was a relief.

"Maybe that had something to do with the way we met," I suggested and David started to laugh.

"And you know," he went on, "because some people think you're stupid, they figure they can rip you off. Make sure you count your change carefully when you buy anything. And now let's get to that store you want."

I started across the concourse of the mall. It was less crowded on this floor, but there were enough people, shopping carts, strollers, and displays to make the way difficult. I had to thread my way around the obstacles. Now I was even more aware that we were being watched. Heads turned as we passed. Once I caught sight of a small boy pointing at us. His mother grabbed him by the arm and spun him around, hoping I hadn't noticed.

Up ahead I saw the store I was looking for —

Kitchen Krafts. I wanted to get there quickly, where it would at least be more private. I pumped harder and picked up speed. Coming to the entrance of the store, I swung in but miscalculated the turn. The chair bumped heavily into a display of pots by the cash register. Desperately, I clutched and grabbed at the tumbling pots filling my arms and my lap, but a few escaped and clattered noisily to the floor and bounced and skittered away.

As the echo of the last bouncing pot faded to silence, I realized that all the other sounds had stopped; there was no conversation or laughter or shuffling of feet. Nervously I looked up. People in the store and in the mall had all stopped and were staring at me. I sank lower into the chair, wanting to fade right through the floor.

"What happened?" an angry voice called out, breaking the silence. "What happened?" A sales lady rushed out, only her head and shoulders visible above a shelf. She saw the pots scattered across the floor and her sharp gaze became even angrier.

"I-I'm s-sorry," I stammered.

"Well, sorry isn't good enough!" she snapped angrily as she marched around the shelf and toward me.

Suddenly she stopped dead in her tracks and her expression changed to shock, and then confusion. "You're . . . you're . . ." She was obviously searching for the right words.

"Sorry, really sorry," I repeated emphatically.

"Are you all right?" She rushed to my side.

"I'm fine, but what about the pots?"

"Don't worry about them. No harm done," she replied as she and a few of the people who had been watching started to pick up the fallen pots. I couldn't help but notice that a couple were dented!

"I was just coming in to buy my mom a birthday present, and I guess I was moving too fast," I explained.

"Isn't that nice, buying your mother a present," the sales woman said.

She took the remaining pots off my lap and piled them haphazardly on the display table. "There, that's the last of them. Now let me help you with that present," she said sweetly.

* * *

"Thanks a lot," I said as the sales woman pushed me clear of the store and into the concourse of the mall. In my lap sat a bright orange Kitchen Kraft bag containing my mom's present.

"Come again, dear, anytime."

I smiled and nodded. There was less chance of me ever appearing in that store again than there was of me sprouting wings and flying. It was bad enough knocking over the pots, but even worse being wheeled around the store like some toddler in a grocery cart. My chair didn't fit down some of the aisles, and more than once she banged my legs on the display shelves. And the whole time she was talking to me in a slow, loud voice. It was awful! In my desperation to get the heck out of the store I just grabbed some salad servers. My mom already had some but I didn't care. All I wanted was to leave.

"Now wasn't that fun?" David asked.

"For who?"

"Well, for me, for starters."

The whole time I'd been in the store David sat out front in the mall. Each time I was pushed to the top of an aisle, I saw him sitting there, smirking.

"I've got to use the can," David said. "Do you have to go?"

"No," I lied. I certainly wasn't going to try to negotiate my chair into a handicapped washroom stall!

"You can wait for me here or just outside the washroom," he suggested.

"I'll come along," I offered. It would be easier to just sit here and wait — and my arms could really use the rest — but I didn't like the thought of being on my own.

We traveled along to the end of the mall and entered a big department store. The aisles here were a lot wider than in the Kitchen Kraft store, and I easily moved around without upsetting anything. The washrooms were at the back of the store. David disappeared into the men's, and I took up a spot by the doors and waited. There was a constant stream of people going into the washrooms. People looked at me, but just like before, when I made eye contact with them, they quickly looked away. And in those split seconds before they looked away I often caught glimpses of sadness, but something else as well. It was like they were looking at me with . . . with . . . I just couldn't find the word.

"Sean!"

The voice broke my thoughts and I turned. It was Mrs. Leigh, my neighbor from down the street. She'd just come out of the women's washroom.

"My God, whatever happened to you?" she asked in a pleading voice.

"Nothing. Nothing happened."

"But you're in a wheelchair!" she said, sounding both shocked and confused.

"Yeah, but I'm okay, really. It's a . . . a . . . school project," I said, impressed with my lie. "I'm experiencing what it's like to be in a wheelchair. It's for a social science assignment."

"That's very . . . interesting," she said, sounding even more confused. "The important thing is that you're okay."

"I'm fine," I assured her.

"You nearly frightened the daylights out of me.

When I saw you in that wheelchair I just naturally thought the worst. I can just imagine how awful it would be to be trapped in a chair, especially for a young man."

"I'm okay, really. It's just for school," I reassured her again.

"Well, thank goodness. I better get going. Say hello to your mother for me," she added. She reached down and squeezed me by the arm and then walked off.

Suddenly David appeared at my side.

"She's right about one thing," David said. "It is like being in a *trap*." He pumped his chair and moved past me.

I hurried after him. "Wait up!"

He stopped and spun around. "I'll meet you at the front door."

"What do you mean, 'meet me?'" I asked.

"Because you're going to take the elevator."

"We both have to take the elevator."

"Not me," he answered.

I was struck by the sickening thought that he was going to try to make it down the stairs again. "You're not going to . . ." I let the sentence fade away.

"Take the stairs?" He read my mind.

I nodded.

"That would be crazy," he said and I felt relieved. "I'm going to take the escalator," he continued.

"You're going to what?" I asked in shock.

"Take the escalator. It's right over here," he said as he started off again.

I was so stunned I didn't know what to say. What was he trying to do, kill himself?

"David!" I yelled out as he disappeared around a high display. Clumsily I hurried after him. Rounding the corner I saw him at the top of the escalator.

"David, you can't!"

He smirked at me. "*You* can't, but I can."

"Don't, please . . . you'll get hurt . . . badly," I said as my eyes focused on the sharp metal edges of the moving steps.

He laughed. "How much more badly do you think I could get hurt?" he asked.

I didn't know what to answer.

"Besides, it's important for you to solo for a while."

"Couldn't we stay together?" I pleaded.

"I don't think so. It's way too difficult for you to even try the escalator, and there's no way I'm going to be *trapped* in that elevator." He spat the word "trapped" out like it was poison.

Before I could utter another syllable, he pushed forward. The chair clattered over the edge and onto the first flattened step. As the step started to drop away, he leaned far back against the seat and slammed the locks on both wheels. The chair balanced on the locked back wheels, while the front wheels dangled over the edge of the step. David grabbed hold of the escalator's handrails as he glided down. My mind was filled with the terrifying image of him tipping off the step and both he and the chair rolling and bashing and crashing down the steps, landing in a bloody heap at the bottom. I held my breath and prayed and waited, then he leaned forward and the chair started to tip over. *Clank*, it hit the bottom step and noisily rolled off the escalator and onto the landing at the bottom. David pushed himself out and away, spun around, and waved up at me.

"Don't even think about it! I'll meet you at the front door!" he yelled before turning and starting off to our meeting spot.

For a split second, I thought about following him. What was the worst thing that could happen? My mind was again filled with the images of a wheelchair tumbling end over end down the escalator, except this time I was the passenger, and then I thought about how I might then spend a lot longer in a chair than I wanted. I violently turned myself away from the escalator like I was somehow afraid it might reach out and grab me.

Chapter 18

"What took you so long?" David asked.

"It's a long way," I offered as an excuse.

I didn't tell him I'd stopped to rest for a couple of minutes. My arms were aching badly and I needed a break.

At one point, as I moved slowly along the mall, I had the overwhelming urge to get up out of the chair and push it. But I didn't. Partly it was because I was nervous about what people would think or do if they suddenly saw me jump up out of my chair. Partly I didn't do it because it wouldn't have been right. If David could live his life in that chair, the least I could do was manage a few hours.

"You really surprised me with that escalator. I was afraid you were going to fall."

"That makes two of us. The end came just in time . . . I was starting to wobble and almost tipped over."

"Have you ever got hurt doing that?" I asked.

"No, never." He paused and a big smile spread across his face. "But then again, that was the first time I ever tried it."

My mouth dropped open. "You're joking."

"No, but I once saw this guy do it."

"And you thought you'd want to try it some day?" I asked.

"No, I thought he was an idiot for even trying it. But today I saw the escalator staring out at me, daring me, and I figured I had to give it a shot."

"But what if it didn't work?"

"Then I'd fall down. No big deal."

"It is a big deal!" I objected. "You could have gotten badly smashed up, even worse than with the stairs."

"I could have, but I didn't. Are you hungry?"

"What?" I asked. I'd heard the words, but blurted out my answer before waiting to think them through.

"Do . . . you . . . want . . . to . . . get . . . food?" David asked, slowly and with an exaggerated voice. "Apparently people do get stupid when they sit in a chair."

"Shut up!" I snapped.

He laughed. "That's more like it. So do you want food?"

I didn't know if David was actually hungry or just wanted to change the subject. I didn't care. I really was hungry. "Yeah, I guess."

"Good, my favorite place isn't far from here. Matter of fact, it's right on the way home." He pushed the button to open the automatic doors.

The ache in my arms didn't seem as strong as the hunger in my stomach. I reached down and pumped for all I was worth to try to keep up with David. He stopped in front of a Wendy's restaurant and rolled into the parking lot. Suddenly David veered away from the entrance.

"Where are you going?" I yelled as I rushed after him.

"The drive-through window," he hollered back, then spun his chair and waited for me to catch him. "I figure the service will be faster out here, we don't have to fight through doors, and, besides, we are 'driving through,' aren't we?"

"But are you sure they'll serve us?"

"I've never tried it before, but this is a day for firsts and there's only one way to find out. Come on."

David pulled up behind a car waiting in the drive-through lane, and I came up beside him, sort of like he was the driver and I was in the passenger seat.

"Order what you want. I'm paying," David said.

"I always get the single combo. Lettuce, onions, and bacon on the burger and a Coke to drink."

The guy ahead of us yelled out his order and drove on to the next window.

"Here we go," David said. "And one more thing. Try to sound like a car, okay?"

We rolled into position and stopped beside the speaker.

"Can I take your order?" asked a metallic voice.

"Yeah," David said, lowering his voice to sound older. "Two single combos, both with Cokes, one burger with everything, and one with just lettuce, onions, and bacon."

"Your total comes to eight dollars and ninety-four cents. Please drive to the second window."

David flashed me a big smile and we rolled forward. I was grateful I was on the "passenger" side and didn't have to talk, or hand the money, to the cashier. We came to a stop and the window slid open.

"That will be eight dollars and . . ." The girl's mouth closed as her eyes widened in wonder.

"And ninety-four cents," David said as he pulled a ten-dollar bill out of his wallet. He reached over to the window to give her the money, but she pulled back her hand as if he was offering her poison.

"You can't come through the drive-through," she sputtered.

"Why not?" David asked.

"Because . . . because you can't! It's just for cars."

"You mean you can't come through here in a truck or a van or on a motorcycle?" David questioned.

"Of course, you can."

"Well, we're just another type of vehicle."

She looked like she didn't know what to think. "I've got to get the manager," she blurted out and the window slid shut.

A car pulled up close behind us. I could feel the heat from the engine pulsing through the air at us. This wasn't looking good. The window slid open again and an older man appeared.

"Hi, boys. We have your food waiting for you inside," he said. His voice was very gentle and he sounded nice.

"Maybe we'd have come inside if you had doors that were wheelchair accessible!" David snapped.

The man looked away, like he'd been caught doing something wrong.

"Anyway, we don't want to come inside. We ordered at the drive-through window because we want to drive through," David said.

The manager heaved a big sigh. "It's not my doing, boys, it's safety rules. We can't allow non-motorized vehicles like bicycles to use the drive- through window."

"Do these look like bicycles?" David demanded. "Does it look like we're out for a little spin on our bikes?

"No, of course not. I just meant we can't

encourage non-motorized vehicles to use the drive-through window. It's dangerous. What if you got hit by a car?"

"Oh, that would be terrible. I could end up injured or in a wheelchair . . . oops, too late for that!" David laughed bitterly.

The man looked taken aback. "Please try to be reasonable. Look at all the people you're holding up," he said, gesturing behind us. I turned around and saw the first car had been joined by a second, and a third, and a fourth. The driver directly behind us glared angrily through his windshield.

"I'm not holding up anybody," David said. "You're the one holding them up by not giving us our food!"

I wasn't feeling so defiant. "Maybe we should go," I suggested quietly to David. I wasn't sure where all this was leading, and I didn't want to find out.

"You leave if you want, but I'm not going anywhere!" he hissed at me. He turned back to the manager. "If you want me to move, give me my food. If not, you're going to have to come out here and move me yourself!"

"Son, this isn't funny."

I reached over and grabbed David's arm. "Come on, we better go."

"No one's stopping you from leaving! You can just stand up and walk away if that's what you want!" he snarled, shaking his arm free of my grip.

I looked over at David and saw that familiar stubborn look. The only way he was going to leave this spot was either with his food or with a fistfight.

"Come on, son, I'm not fooling around," the manager said.

"He's not fooling around, either!" I blurted out. "If he says he isn't going to move, he isn't going to move!"

David solemnly nodded his head in agreement and I felt a rush of determination.

"And I'm not moving, either," I said through clenched teeth. "So give us our food or come on out and try to *make* us move!"

The man looked like he wanted to say something — his mouth opened and closed repeatedly — but no words came out. He disappeared inside and the window slid shut once again.

"Good speech," David said. "Did you mean it?"

"Yeah . . . I guess . . . most of it. Do you think he's coming out?"

"I'd like to see him try."

I was suddenly struck by the thought that David actually hoped the man *would* try to move us. He probably wanted that with the same intensity that I hoped it wouldn't happen.

The window slid open once again and a bag was thrust through. "Here's your order," the cashier said.

David took the bag and placed it in his lap.

"And here's your money."

Hastily she took the bill, made change, and handed it back to him.

"Thanks." Slowly he put the coins in his wallet and stuffed it in his front pocket. "Maybe we should check our order before we leave," he suggested.

"Are you crazy?" I asked in disbelief.

He smiled. "Just fooling around." Slowly he started moving like he was in no rush. If he'd been walking instead of rolling, I would have said he was swaggering, the way you might move after a big play, or at the end of a game where your team blew the other side away.

He turned left, toward home, at the sidewalk, and I fell in behind.

David looked over his shoulder. "Thanks for backing me."

"That's okay," I shrugged, "anytime."

The words had hardly escaped my lips when I thought that that was a particularly risky thing to say to David — anytime could be only moments away.

I had never known anybody could put himself so squarely in front of trouble so often. He had said that his mother had described him as "careless," and I had thought that maybe she was right. Now I was beginning to think that it wasn't the right word. "Careless" seemed like somebody who stumbled into things without thinking them through, and that wasn't David. It wasn't that things just happened to him, but that he went out of his way to look for something, and if he couldn't see it, he'd build it himself. He wasn't careless. He was reckless.

"Here we are," David announced.

"Where?"

"Where we're going to eat."

It was the old spark-plug factory, which had been closed down for years. It was three stories of crumbling red brick. Last year we'd made up really scary stuff about ghosts or murderers living inside.

"But we can't go in there!" I protested.

"We're not going inside. We'll eat in the back. There's a nice place to sit."

We rolled along the driveway. It was marked by large potholes and cracks in the pavement, some of which were filled with grass and knee high weeds. We circled to the side of the building, and our way was blocked by a high chain-link fence and a gate secured with a large chain and lock.

"This is the nice place you want to eat?" I questioned.

David cocked a finger for me to follow, and he cruised down the length of the fence. He stopped in front of a small hole in the chain-link.

"You don't think we can get through that, do you?" I asked.

"No, but I do think we can get through this," David answered. He leaned forward and took hold of the fence. A large section peeled away from the poles.

"Who did that?" I asked.

"I watched some kids with dirt bikes fooling around in the parking lot a couple of times, and I saw them go through the fence. After they left I tried it myself."

"I know a few guys who ride their bikes in the gorge behind here," I said.

"Gorge?"

"Yeah, it's down the way, although I haven't come at it from this direction," I admitted.

"I've never gone very far down the path. Maybe we should explore a bit," David suggested.

"In these?" I said, without thinking.

David shot me an angry glare. I held my breath and waited for his response. Instead he said nothing. David rolled back, holding the fence until the opening became large enough for me to fit through. As soon as I'd cleared it, he came after me, moving the chair back and forth to neatly seal the opening up again. I was impressed by how he maneuvered the chair. David again took the lead and aimed for the back corner of the parking lot where there was another large hole in the fence.

"They did a good job with these holes," I said.

"Yeah, really neat. I figure they used either a big set of bolt cutters or a hacksaw."

We went through the second hole and bumped onto a narrow gravel path that split a grassy flat.

"Where are we going to eat?" I asked.

"I had thought we'd stop right here, but now that I know there's a gorge farther along I think we should go and eat there."

I instantly knew that this was his way of getting back at me for what I'd said. I wanted to say something, tell him I wasn't coming with him, but I was helpless. I followed behind, bumping and bouncing down the path. It was hard to move straight as the wheels kept on getting caught in the gravel.

Soon I could hear the sound of rushing water. On the far edge of the grass, trees and bushes blocked my view of what I knew was far below — the river rushing by. Anxiously I followed behind David as he traveled the thin strip between the fence and the brush. Even though the ground was flat, I had to work much harder to move. There was no glide — I had to pump on the wheels or I wouldn't move. David came to a stop and I struggled to his side.

"What do you think of the view?" David asked.

The underbrush had dropped away and the thin strip of grass was now only a dozen feet from a jagged drop-off. I didn't need to get any closer to know the river was running below us, far below us. I clicked the locks on both wheels.

"Here." David said handing me the fries, burger, and Coke. "They're not hot, but they're still warm."

I stuck the drink between my legs while I unwrapped the burger and dumped the fries onto the wrapper beside it. I took a big bite of the burger. It was only slightly warm but it tasted even better than usual, which probably said more about how hungry I was. I never would have figured that sitting down all day could work up such an appetite. I polished it all off in two minutes flat.

"You're not afraid of heights, are you?" David asked.

"No . . . not really," I answered. That was only partially a lie because how I felt went way beyond afraid and all the way to terrified.

I once went on an outing with my family to a scenic tower. It was bad enough that it was really high and we had to take a glass-sided elevator to the top, but when we reached the top, I saw that a section of the floor was glass! People were taking turns walking across it, looking down through their shoes to the ground five hundred feet below. I stood far off to the side and watched as first my father and mother and Janice and then finally the Boo Boos walked over it. I could barely stand to watch. Each time my knees got weak and a series of shivers radiated along my spine until they settled uneasily into my stomach.

Things would have been okay if Janice hadn't started to get on my case. She began to tease me about how even the Boo Boos weren't afraid and what a little chicken I was. Finally, feeling I had no choice, I joined the line of people waiting for their turn to cross the small section of floor. As I waited, shuffling slowly forward, I tried to convince myself it would be all right. I knew that it was special glass, probably so thick and strong it could hold an elephant. Despite my head knowing it was safe, my legs were in disagreement and locked at the edge of the glass, refusing to go forward. I'd just stopped for a few seconds when I could hear grumbling and complaints coming from behind me. Over to the side I caught sight of my family watching — my sister snickering. I had no choice. I closed my eyes and stepped forward out onto the glass. And that was when it happened . . . I threw up all over the glass floor.

It was a colorful and goopy mixture of popcorn, hot dog covered with mustard and ketchup, and pink candy floss. I was never so embarrassed in my life, and I think my family knew it. Even my sister, after she got over the initial round of laughter, never mentioned it to me again.

David rolled his chair forward. As he neared the edge I leaned back in my chair, as if I could somehow counterbalance him.

"It's a long way down," David said.

"I believe that."

"You should see the view from here."

"I can see good from where I am," I answered.

"There's a path leading down. It's not very wide and it's bumpy and really, really steep. Do you want to try going down it?"

"You can't be serious!" I blurted out.

David laughed. "I was just kidding. It would be suicidal to try to get down there in a chair. One slip or dip and you and your chair would go tumbling down the cliff and would smash to smithereens on the rocks at the bottom." He paused. "You know, that's what I'm going to do with this chair when I don't need it anymore. I'm going to take it right here and heave it off the side of this cliff. Maybe I'll even videotape it smashing and crashing as it tumbles down to the bottom! That would be amazingly cool!"

"It would be cool — especially the part about you not needing the chair anymore."

"And then right after I toss the chair, I'll walk up the stairs leading to the Howard Gardiner Center."

"The what?" I asked.

"Howard Gardiner. It's the rehabilitation place, you know, the hospital, where I lived after the accident. All sorts of nurses and doctors and physiotherapists and occupational therapists and social workers and other people are there."

"Social workers?" I asked, remembering what David's mother said.

"Yeah, they were always bugging me about how I feel," he said, shaking his head. "How would you feel if you were in a wheelchair?"

Did he want me to answer that?

"And even now — I've been gone from that place over six months — this one social worker still calls every few weeks, 'just to see how I'm doing.' Can you believe that?"

"I guess they're just worried," I suggested hesitantly.

"I don't need people worrying about me!" he snapped and then turned away.

I sat there, unsure what to say, but feeling like I had to say something. "How long were you at the rehab center?"

"A little under six months."

"That's a long time. What was it like?"

"It was . . . it was . . ." He turned his chair away from the river to face me. "It was awful."

"Were the people . . . okay?" I asked.

"Everybody tried to be nice."

I could see the strain in his face and anguish in his eyes.

"That's where I smashed all my trophies." He looked over at me, trying to judge my reaction. "I guess you're wondering how I could do that."

I nodded. The image of the broken and smashed trophies flashed in my mind. I hadn't completely been able to escape them since that night.

"I wish I knew . . . but I really don't," he said softly. "I remember winning each and every one of them. And then, when my parents brought them to the hospital, it just sort of happened. One minute I'm sitting alone in my room looking at them and the next I just picked one up and snapped off the top. And then I did the same with another, and another, and another, until they were all broken."

"Maybe you can get them fixed," I offered.

"That's what my mother said, but I guess I don't want them fixed." He sniffled and there was a catch in his voice.

"You don't have to talk about this stuff."

"No," he said, shaking his head. "It's okay."

"It must have been hard living in a hospital that long," I said, trying to steer the conversation away from the trophies.

"It was hard, especially at first. There was so much to deal with . . ." A shudder went through his entire body. "And I kept hoping that somehow the whole thing was just a bad dream . . . a nightmare. It was so hard to accept . . . it's still so hard . . . especially at night. For months after the accident I'd wake up in the middle of the night and be in a panic."

"That would be terrible."

"And do you want to know the very worst part?"

Every part seemed like the worst part. I nodded.

"One night I woke up and it all came back to me in a rush . . . my legs . . . everything. And then somehow, I'm not sure why, I became calm because I knew none of it could be real. It was nothing more than a terrible, awful, bad nightmare. I just knew I was in my own bed in my own house with my mom and dad sleeping in their room down the hall. And the whole thing seemed so silly that I wanted to go and see them and tell them all about my nightmare. And when I tried to move I couldn't. My legs wouldn't move. And then I switched on the light on the nightstand and I saw the chair . . . the chair I'm sitting in right now . . . and it was like the whole thing happened over again."

David was fighting to hold the tears back and he turned away. I turned away as well. Somehow it seemed better that I didn't see him cry — and that he didn't see me cry, either.

Chapter 19

"Well?" I asked.

"Well what?" David replied.

"Did you ask her?"

"Not yet."

"It's Monday, the dance is only four days away, you know."

"I have the days of the week figured out," he snapped. "I'm aware that Friday is four days after Monday." He paused. "So, what did Caroline say when you asked her."

"I didn't ask her yet, either," I mumbled.

"Hah! And you're giving me a hard time! When were you planning on asking her?"

"I *was* planning on asking her this past weekend."

"And what happened?" David asked.

"I called her . . . twice."

"And?"

"And we talked. We even talked about the dance."

"And?" he asked again.

"And every time I went to ask her, the words got stuck in my throat."

David shook his head, tucked his hands under his armpits, and started to flap his arms and make chicken sounds.

"I'm not a chicken . . . about most things," I admitted. "It's just that it's hard enough for me to talk to girls anyway. Not like you."

He shrugged. "What's so hard? It's just like talking to guys."

"No, it isn't."

"Girls are just like guys, except for different body parts," David explained.

I couldn't help but laugh.

"I remember the first time I asked a girl to a dance and —"

"You've done this before?"

"Sure, lots of times."

"And they said yes?"

"Funny," David said. "Real funny."

"I wasn't trying to be funny. I just wanted to know what it would be like if I was turned down."

David smiled. "Can't help you there."

"You've never been turned down?"

He shook his head and the smile became bigger.

"Now I'm confused," I said.

"You're confused that I've never been turned down? Gee, thanks for the vote of confidence!"

"Not that," I said. "I know why I'm nervous about asking Caroline . . . I've never asked anybody to a dance before. But you?"

David stopped smiling. "It's different now."

Of course, I knew what he meant. He asked those girls before . . . before the accident . . . before he was in the chair.

"How about if we make a deal?" I asked.

He just looked at me. "Go on."

"We both ask before the end of the day."

"School day or real day?" he asked.

"Real day. I might have to wait until tonight, on the phone. Deal?"

David looked like he was thinking. Suddenly he reached out his hand.

"Deal," he said and we shook.

* * *

I threw my books in my locker with a loud thud and grabbed my gym bag. I had to get to the gym. This was the last week of tryouts. I'd spent all afternoon rehearsing in my head what I'd say to Caroline. I still wasn't sure if I had it right, but I knew that I couldn't delay it anymore. Right after basketball practice I'd go straight home and call her — first thing, no delay, no waiting.

"Hi, Sean."

I spun around to see Caroline standing there, alone.

"How are you?" I asked.

"I'm fine. And you?"

"Um . . . I'm good, I guess."

"That's good," she answered.

There was a painful silence. I felt sweat start to drip down my sides.

"Are you going to basketball practice?" she asked.

"Yeah. And you?"

"Waiting for Lisa. She had to get some extra help in math."

"I see," I said, nodding my head.

More painful silence. Seconds of it. I had to ask her. I had to get up the nerve to just spit out the words.

"Are you going to the dance on Friday?" Caroline asked.

"Yeah!" I said, nodding my head enthusiastically. "I actually wanted to talk to you about that."

"You did?" she asked.

I took a deep breath. "Yeah . . . I was wondering if you'd go with me to the —"

"I'd love to!" she exclaimed.

I let out my breath. I felt a wave of anxiety instantly replaced by a rush of pure happiness. Boy, did that feel good.

"But you'll have to come to my house first," she continued.

"Sure, I can do that, I guess," I said.

"Because my father wants to meet you."

"Meet me?" I suddenly felt anxious again.

"He said he wanted to anyway, because you've called the house, and now there's no way he'd let me go out on a date without meeting the boy."

A date . . . that sounded strange . . . I was going out on a date.

"Maybe you could come over about half an hour before the dance," Caroline suggested. "I bet my father will even drive us there."

"That'll be great . . . will there be space enough for David?" I asked.

There was a pause. "Lisa's coming, too."

"Well, of course, she's coming," I said.

There was another pause. "I just don't know if it would be comfortable."

"Why, isn't your father's car very big?"

"I don't mean comfortable that way. I mean with Lisa turning him down when he asked her to the dance."

"She turned him down?"

"She felt bad about it," Caroline said.

"Then why did she do it?"

"It's just that, I don't know what to say. Maybe you better ask her yourself," Caroline said as she motioned down the hall.

I turned around to see Lisa walking toward us. She waved and gave us a big smile. "There that didn't take too long I —"

"Why aren't you going with David to the dance?" I demanded, cutting her off and wiping the smile off her face.

"I . . . I just —"

"I thought you liked him!"

"I do like him," she answered.

"You have a funny way of showing it!"

"It's just that I don't like him *that* way."

"What do you mean *that* way?" I demanded.

"It's just that . . . that . . ." Suddenly she burst into tears, turned, and ran up the hall.

I turned back to Caroline. "I didn't mean to make her cry."

"You hurt her feelings!" she snapped, defending her friend.

"Well, she hurt David's feelings, badly . . . I'm sure," I protested.

"Lisa said he took it okay," Caroline said.

"He did?"

Caroline nodded. "She told me he just said 'fine, see you later,' and left. If you're worried, maybe you should call him."

"I guess I could." The thought of making that call made me more apprehensive than meeting Caroline's father.

"It's just that it's a dance and Lisa loves to dance."

"So does David."

"I mean really dance. Do you think David knows that's why she turned him down?"

"I don't know," I said, but, of course, he would know that it had something to do with him being in a chair.

"You could talk to him at school tomorrow at lunch . . . but I guess you can't because Lisa and Christina will be there, too. That'll be okay, won't it, us all still eating lunch together?"

"I wish I knew," I said, shaking my head.

Life had suddenly gotten a lot more complicated than I had wanted.

Chapter 20

"Here you go, Sean, dinner is served!" David's father said as he put a plate in front of me.

"Um, thanks . . . it looks . . . interesting." I had absolutely no idea what it was.

"That's a good word for it," David said. "Interesting."

"It does look a little different, but you didn't come here to *look*, you came here to *eat*. Try it!" Tiny said.

"Sure," I answered, and then paused, the fork partway up to my mouth. "What is it?"

"He won't tell you," David answered. "And if you're smart you don't even want to know. Some of the things I've enjoyed the most I never would have eaten if he'd told me what they were before

I put a forkful in my mouth."

"Like what?" I asked anxiously.

"Calves' brains, for one," David answered.

I cringed and everybody noticed and laughed.

"No, really, it's wonderful! Then there was tongue and eel and pickled herring and —"

"Enough talk. Have a mouthful. I'll guarantee you'll like it!" Tiny stated loudly.

I didn't like arguing with somebody who was big enough to eat *me* in one meal. "This isn't brains, is it?" I asked weakly.

His father gave me a menacing look, which dissolved into a smile. I knew he was just fooling around, but when he stared at me like that I would have been prepared to eat just about anything.

"No, there's not a brain in there. It's meat . . . mystery meat," he chuckled.

"This is good," David piped up. "Very good."

He put another piece in his mouth, chewed, and swallowed. "I don't quite know how to describe it, but, really, you should try it. You'll like it."

I was hoping this meal would be more comfortable than the last three lunches I'd shared with David — along with Caroline, Christina, and Lisa. David hadn't said much about being turned down to go to the dance. He was trying his best to act like it didn't bother him, but I knew it did. It had to. I just hoped it would all blow over and things would go back to the way they were before.

"So are you going to try it or just stare at it?"

Tiny asked.

"Try it, I guess," I answered.

I lifted up my fork and grimaced slightly. My arms were still a bit sore, a full five days after my day in the wheelchair. But they were better than the day after when I could hardly put on my socks. I opened wide and bit down on the food. It had a strange texture to it, but it tasted good — sort of sweet and tangy. I tried to think of what it reminded me of. The closest thing that came to mind was that it felt like I was biting into bubble gum; it had a little bit of a bouncy or rubbery feeling.

"Well?" David asked.

"I like it," I said, although part of me was prepared to say I liked it no matter what. That wasn't just being polite. Despite everything David had said about his father being friendly and gentle, he still spooked me.

"Good. Take a couple more bites."

"Sure, no problem." I took another forkful, this time much larger than the first. "Can you tell me what it is now?"

"Calamari," David's father smiled.

"I've never even heard of it. What's calamari?" I asked as I shoveled in more of the meal.

"Squid."

I stopped chewing. "Squid?" I asked through a mouthful of food.

"Yeah. Nothing like fresh squid. These babies were swooshing around in a tank less than three hours ago," David's mother said.

Somehow I didn't like the idea of anything I ate doing any "swooshing," ever.

"I picked them up for my husband," she continued. "It's part of our arrangement. I do the shopping and he does the cooking."

"Aren't you glad he didn't tell you what it was before you tried it?" David asked.

"I guess so," I admitted reluctantly. If he hadn't told me at all, though, I wouldn't be trying to figure out now if I could get away with spitting out the rest into my napkin. Looking around at the eyes focused on me, I knew that wasn't an option. I swallowed hard and prayed it wouldn't come back up. Then I reached for the pitcher of milk to replenish my glass and wash down the squid.

"So how was your wheelchair adventure the other day?" David's father asked.

That caught me by surprise. I didn't realize they even knew about it.

"David mentioned it to us. How did it go?" his mother asked.

"It was interesting."

"Isn't that the same word you used to describe this meal?" David asked.

I smiled. "Yeah. I guess the two have a lot in common. Just like with the squid," I said, lifting up my fork, "if I'd known what I was getting into before I did it, I probably wouldn't have done it."

"Why, what happened?" Tiny asked.

I could tell by the way both his parents had stopped eating that this was more than a casual question.

"Oh, nothing much," I said.

David gave me a slight nod to acknowledge his appreciation for all the things he knew I wasn't going to say.

"Something must have happened," his mother pressed me for more.

"Well . . . it was different. I learned a lot about going across roads and how difficult it is to get around stores and, of course, there was the escalator —"

"The escalator? What about an escalator?" his mother asked suspiciously. David shot me a concerned look.

"I learned to avoid them!" I said quickly. "They're really dangerous when you're in a chair. David helped me to understand how to do things the safe way!"

"I'm glad David knows the safe way to do things, even if he doesn't always do it," she said pointedly. "Escalators are probably even more dangerous than long sets of stairs." She was talking to me, but the words were aimed at David.

"Did you learn anything else?" David's father asked.

I nodded. "A lot." I had spent hours and hours thinking about all the things that had happened.

I wasn't sure where to begin. There were some things I was willing to talk about, some I wasn't, and a bunch more that were still just too jumbled and confusing to even try to make sense of. "You know, it wasn't so much about being in the chair that I learned about, but how people reacted to me being in the chair. People treat you different. They act like you're . . . you're . . ."

"Stupid!" David snapped.

"I know you always say that," his mother said, "but *I've* never seen anybody treat you badly."

David looked like he was going to say something, but I jumped in first.

"Nobody treated me badly," I said.

She gave David a smug smile.

"A couple of times it was the opposite. They treated me well even when I'd done something wrong."

"Like when you smashed up those pots," David said.

"You smashed up some pots?" his mother asked in amazement.

I nodded. I still felt embarrassed about that incident. "Not on purpose," I quickly replied. "It's just that there was this sort of display and I didn't exactly see it, and I bumped it with my chair and it sort of slid over."

"Slid over!" David exclaimed. "It practically exploded! Pots went skittering along the floor halfway across the store!"

"Yeah, I guess a couple of them shot off a bit," I reluctantly admitted. "But did you see how that sales lady treated me?"

"She must have cursed you out good," Tiny said.

"She started to," I said. "Until she saw I was in a chair. She stopped yelling and couldn't do enough to help me."

"And why is this a problem?" David's mother asked.

"It's because they feel sorry for you," I added.

"But how do you know that's how they feel?"

"I don't know . . . it's sort of the way they look at you. You can see it in their eyes. It's a look of . . . a look of . . ." I still hadn't been able to fill in the blank.

"Pity," David said. "I see it in people's eyes all the time." He paused. "Sometimes I see it in yours," he said to his parents.

They both looked down at their plates, and we all sat in silence for what seemed like a long time. Somebody had to break the silence.

"They're going to name the school basketball team tomorrow. I hope I make it," I said.

"We'll keep our fingers crossed," David's mother said.

"Don't waste your time," David declared. "He's on the team for sure."

"I had some help with that."

David smiled. "No problem. I'd much rather

play than coach, but at least it keeps me around the gym."

"Well, I guess you can coach until you can play again. I figure we'll be on the same team before the end of high school," I said.

"What do you mean?" His mother looked confused.

"Maybe sooner. With the way spinal cord research is going, I'm sure we'll be playing together in three or four years."

"Did David tell you that?" she asked.

"He told me a lot and we did a school project on it . . . of course, David did most of that part, but he was able to explain it all to me."

His parents exchanged a look of concern. I looked over at David for help, but he was staring down at his plate. I suddenly felt very uncomfortable.

"We all hope that someday the research will make a difference. It's just that it's still so experimental," his mother said.

"I don't understand," I said.

"The research they're doing on spinal regeneration is just in the very, very beginning stages."

"But they're making great progress," I said, echoing words David had said to me.

"Yes, they are, but that progress is very slow. It may be twenty or even thirty years before it could actually benefit people and —"

"Or two years or tomorrow!" David interrupted angrily. "Sometimes things happen overnight like that!"

His mother sighed and took a deep breath. "Yes, sometimes they do happen more quickly. And we all pray for that, but you can hold up your life waiting." She paused. "Isn't that what the social workers told you?"

"It doesn't matter what they said," David snapped. "The breakthrough is coming, even if it does take a few years."

It felt like somebody had kicked me in the stomach. Imagine having to deal with all this, as well as being turned down by Lisa. It had been so hard talking to him about Lisa's rejection, but I guess that really didn't mean much compared to other things.

I glanced over at David sitting beside me. There was a large wet patch on his pants, and something was dripping from the side of his chair and onto the floor. Had he spilled something on himself? David looked up at me, and then his eyes followed my gaze to his lap. He raised his eyes to mine again, and his face was a mixture of sadness and shock and embarrassment.

"I've got to go!" David blurted out as he spun his chair around and pumped out of the room, leaving behind a thin, wet trail.

"Oh, that's awful!" his mother said. She turned to her husband. "Go and help him, please."

He nodded and then quickly got up from the table and hurried down the hall after David.

"That's so embarrassing for David. I hope you won't tell anybody," his mother said.

"Tell them what? I don't understand what happened."

She rose from her seat and came close to my side. "David doesn't have any control over his bladder. It runs into a bag and he has to change it when it's full. The bag must have sprung a leak. David would appreciate it — we'd all appreciate it — if you didn't mention this to anybody."

"I won't, believe me, I won't," I said, shaking my head emphatically.

"I know you won't," she said as she gave my hand a squeeze. "And I'm sorry if it sounded like we were being hard on David about the research, but we have to do that."

"You do?"

She nodded. "They told us if he spends too much time hoping for things that aren't, or may never be, he'll never learn to accept his loss and get on with life. Do you understand?"

"I guess . . . a little."

"It's not easy." She paused. "If you'll excuse me for a minute, I have to go and see if David's all right."

I nodded. Then I sat there with an awful feeling in my gut that had nothing to do with the squid.

Chapter 21

Numbly I gathered up my books and stuffed them into my pack. The room was filled with the noises of talking, laughter, and movement as kids hurried out of class. Over top of everything, the teacher's voice yelled out a warning not to forget our assignment for next class. I had no idea what he was talking about, but that wasn't surprising; I hadn't heard one word that was said throughout the entire class. There was too much going on inside my head to take in anything more.

I gathered up my stuff and stumbled out of the classroom toward the gym. There wasn't a tryout tonight. It was all over and decided. All that was left was for me to go and check out the bulletin board outside the gym. A list of the team would be posted there at four o'clock. I'd been thinking of nothing else all day. Part of me wondered how I'd survive if I didn't make the team. But the biggest part of me questioned how I could let something like that bother me so much. This was just some stupid basketball team — not the rest of my life. I laughed to myself. Just a few short weeks ago making that team seemed like the most important thing in the world. And now? Well, suddenly things took on a different perspective. Whether I made it or not didn't really matter at all . . . not at all. It wasn't big or important like something bad happening to somebody in my family, or somebody dying, or . . . or . . . like having to live my life in a wheelchair. It was just a team.

Last night I kept thinking about what life would be like being in the chair. It was so much more than not being able to get down stairs or play basketball. And I wanted to tell David that I didn't understand it all, and knew that I couldn't — only he knew what he was going through. But what I did know was that something about your legs not working could change everything else.

I had waited for David by his locker before school. I'd waited until the bell sounded and he still hadn't shown, so I hurried to class. I figured that he was just a little late, that I'd see him two periods later in math, or at lunch. But he wasn't in school. Maybe he was sick or had another one of those appointments with a doctor. Or maybe he couldn't bear to face me after what happened at dinner last night.

I really wanted to talk to somebody about things, but I couldn't. I had promised his mother I'd keep quiet, and that promise had to include even my parents.

"Sean, are you all right?"

I stopped and found myself staring at Mr. McCully.

"You look a little lost."

"I'm fine," I mumbled.

"I guess I should offer you my congratulations," he said as he extended his hand.

Without thinking, I reached out my hand and he took it. "Congratulations for what?"

"For making the basketball team." He flashed a big smile.

"I did? But how would you know?" I asked. "The team list isn't going to be posted for another . . ." I looked at my watch, "ten minutes."

Mr. McCully laughed. "There are a few advantages to being the vice-principal. The coach had to clear the list with me to make sure that none of the potential players were barred from the team because of academic or behavior reasons."

"Oh," I said, nodding my head.

"And both your behavior and your marks have been excellent!"

"Thanks," I said flatly.

He looked confused. "I thought you'd be more excited. Making the team is something you really wanted, isn't it?"

"Yeah . . . sure . . . definitely," I replied, trying to feign a little enthusiasm.

"Making the team is something to be proud of, but it seems to me your attitude and actions this year should be a real source of pride — to yourself and your family. You've shown a lot of growth."

"Growth?" I questioned.

"Yes. A new maturity. You've been in absolutely no trouble at all. Have you even been in detention once this year?"

"No, not once."

"Excellent! Well, I have to get going, I've got a few things to attend to and you must want to get home and tell your parents about making the team. I'm sure they'll be even happier for you than I am."

"Yeah, they will be happy," I said. I knew my parents, especially my father, would be thinking about the team being announced today, and I did want to tell them.

We hurried off down the hall in different directions. I tossed my backpack into the locker with a loud thud, grabbed my jacket, and slammed the door closed. The halls were practically empty now. It always amazed me how fast nine hundred kids could scurry out of the exits at the end of the day.

I pushed out through one of the doors and started down the stairs and . . . Scott was sitting on the ramp. I slowed down. Things hadn't been that comfortable between us.

"How's it going?" I asked.

"Been worse, been better," he said.

"I made the team," I blurted out.

"Would have been shocked if you didn't. Want to sit down?" he asked, gesturing to the spot beside him.

"I really don't have . . . sure," I said. I really wanted to get home, but a few minutes here might be all right. I was feeling guiltier about Scott all the time. I sat down beside him and we watched in silence as a few more kids trickled out of the doors and down the stairs.

"You going to the dance tonight?" Scott asked.

"Yeah. You?"

"Thinking about it. Me and the guys," he said. "You could, you know, join us if you wanted."

"I can't. I'm going with somebody else."

"You don't have to go everywhere with him, you know," Scott said, sounding annoyed.

"No," I said, shaking my head, "I don't even think David's coming tonight."

"He's not? Then who are you going with?"

"A girl . . . Caroline."

"That sevener? You'd be seen at the dance with her?"

"She's in grade seven," I said, feeling defensive. "That doesn't mean I can't be seen with her."

"Well, I guess that's a step up from who you're usually hanging around with."

"You're right," I snapped. "It is a big step up from who I hung around with . . . last year."

"Funny," Scott said. "I meant David."

I stood up. "I know what you meant. And I wasn't trying to be funny. I like David and I like Caroline. You? I'm not so sure about anymore."

Scott jumped to his feet. He looked angry. I didn't want to fight him but now that I'd made the team, I could afford a scuffle.

"You used to be fun," Scott said, shaking his head.

"Fun, is that what you call it? I was thinking more like stupid," I said. "And I'm not stupid anymore."

"Are you saying I am?" Scott asked, sounding angrier.

"Forget it Scott. I'd explain it to you, but you're not worth the trouble." Without looking back, I walked away.

Maybe I should have felt bad or upset — Scott *had* been a friend — but I felt relieved, like a weight had been lifted off my shoulders. I bounced down the front steps, taking them three at a time. I suddenly felt a growing sense of excitement. I'd made the team! I picked up my pace.

I thought of a half dozen ways to tell my parents, including pretending I didn't make the team, making them guess, or just acting casual until they asked me. I'd finally decided to just tell them. Seeing the house up ahead gave me a renewed boost of energy, and I sprinted past the last dozen houses. I threw open the door.

"Mom, I made the team!" I yelled.

There was no answer. I walked into the kitchen. It was empty. I peeked out the window to the side of the house and saw that her car wasn't there. Didn't she remember this was the day they were going to announce the team? I needed to tell somebody. Maybe I could call Dad at work? I looked at my watch. It was too late. He'd already left the office and was on his way home. I hoped somebody would be home soon to make something for supper. The dance was in a few hours, and I had to eat and get washed up and dressed and to Caroline's place and . . . I thought about David again.

I wanted to call and tell him that I'd made the team. That would be an excuse to find out if he was okay. Would it be like I was bragging or rubbing it in that I had made the team? I shook my head. Throughout this whole thing he'd never been anything but positive about me playing ball. I grabbed the phone and dialed. It was picked up on the second ring.

"Heeeellloooo," his mother's voice sang out. I could hear loud music twanging away in the background.

"Hi, this is Sean. Can I please speak to David?"

"He's not home, Sean."

I guessed he was at the doctor's or something.

"Can you get him to call me when he gets in? I have big news."

"What could have happened between now and the last time you saw him? It couldn't have been any more than forty minutes ago."

"Forty minutes ago?" I echoed.

"Maybe it was a little bit longer than that. I can never make sense of David's schedule. Did you two have the same last period today?"

"N-not today," I stammered. She thought David had been in school! And if he wasn't at home, where was he?

"Did he say anything to you at lunch?" she asked.

"Nothing," I answered, truthfully. He hadn't said a word because he hadn't been there.

"I was just a little worried. Maybe I shouldn't be saying anything, but I know how close the two of you are. David seemed so upset this morning, worse than I've ever seen him before. I didn't even want to let him go to school, but he seemed to calm down and told me it was important that he go."

"He was upset?" I asked.

"You didn't notice? I'm so glad to hear that you couldn't even tell! I guess David was right. He said he'd be fine and he was."

"Um . . . yeah," I managed to say. I felt trapped. Should I tell her he wasn't in school? If she found out he'd be in big trouble, and I'd be the one who ratted him out. Maybe he just needed some time on his own. He probably just hung at the mall or . . . or . . . he was in some sort of trouble.

"I'll have David call you when he gets home," she said. "He shouldn't be very much longer."

"Sure. That would be good. Bye." I placed the telephone back in the receiver.

My legs suddenly felt tired and I slumped into a chair. He was okay. He had to be okay. But I wasn't convinced. I had a terrible feeling in the pit of my stomach that something was horribly wrong. But what? And what could I possibly do about it even if I knew? It wasn't like I could go out and search the city, scour the streets looking for him. And I didn't have that much time anyway. I had to get ready for the dance. Besides, I didn't even have the vaguest idea where to look . . . or did I?

Chapter 22

I picked my jacket up off the floor and hurried out the door. Out on the porch I hesitated for a moment, thinking I should leave a note, but I couldn't figure out what to write if I did. I hoped I wasn't going to be that long. He was either where I thought he was, and I was going to find him right away, or he wasn't, in which case I'd just turn around and head back home. And I'd still have time to get ready for the dance. Maybe not take a shower, but get ready anyway.

I jumped down the front steps. What would David think about me running out to search for him? He got mad if I even suggested he might need help, or tried to push his chair. I could just imagine how he'd react to this. I certainly wasn't going to tell anybody — especially David — if this was all just in my head. And that's what all this was, just some crazy idea. David could get angry, but he always got himself out of it. He wouldn't do anything drastic . . . would he?

I thought about anger as I ran. Last night as I was trying to get to sleep, the first time I got in trouble last year at Homelands popped into my mind. It was over something stupid and small that wasn't even my fault. But I still got punished. It wasn't fair! It just wasn't fair! And remembering this, I got angry all over again. Then I thought about David. One day he's a basketball star and then the accident happens, and the next thing he remembers is being in the hospital, not able to use his legs. How is any of that fair? Maybe the only thing that was fair was that he had the right to be angry. I think I would have rather died than woken up to all of that . . . would rather be dead.

That thought echoed around in my head, shot down my spine, and settled into my stomach. Is that what he'd been doing on that flight of stairs, or crossing streets without looking, or continually picking fights, or charging down that escalator? I knew he wasn't careless, like his mother thought. I was beginning to think that it wasn't even just being reckless, like I'd believed before. It was more than that. I doubled my pace.

There wasn't a soul in sight as I rounded the front of the deserted factory. Being by myself made it seem even more run-down. Something about the place had always spooked me. I remembered the ghost stories my friends and I used to make up about this place. Deliberately, I turned away from the boarded-up and broken windows. I didn't want to see somebody, or something, looking back at me. I wish I'd never heard any of those stupid, old stories.

I rounded the corner of the building and made for the fence. I couldn't pick out where the opening was at first, but then I saw it. I peeled the fence away and stepped through. I was about to put the fence back in place when I hesitated. I wanted to be able to get out, and quickly, if I found something I didn't like. I shook my head — like the fence would stop some ghost if I ran into one.

Halfway across the parking lot I spied the other big hole in the fence. I ran over to it and stepped through. Following the trail, I looked down at the gravel. There were lots of wheel tracks — dirt bikes and regular bicycles. I couldn't tell if a wheelchair had just rolled by.

I was struck by the near silence. There were no sounds except the wind rustling through the leaves, a few birds twittering, and the rumble of the river far below. There was nothing in sight; not even the birds that I could hear. I felt nervous.

When I was walking someplace, especially at night, I'd often hum a bit or even talk to myself. And when I had to pass by a closed-in space, like a garage, I'd talk out loud. I'd say things like, "Boy

I'm glad to be home after my karate class." Sometimes I'd even talk in two different voices so it sounded like a couple of people having a conversation. That could certainly fool somebody — somebody who wasn't very bright.

Quietly I started to hum as I continued along the trail. It was funny how much more level and even the ground felt now that I was walking instead of rolling. Along one side the trees and bushes were thinning out and then abruptly stopped altogether. The trail traveled straight ahead and then disappeared over the lip of the drop. I felt a rush of apprehension, which left when I realized I wasn't facing it in a chair this time. There wasn't any danger of rolling out of control.

I paused at the very edge of the drop. This was just about the place where David had stopped that day. A low whistle escaped my lips. The trail dropped off sharply and then twisted and turned and snaked its way down the steep slope, dodging behind some bushes until it met a thin, grassy strip shadowing the river.

I was so struck by the view that it took a few seconds to register that David wasn't anywhere in sight. He wasn't there. I felt relief . . . for a few seconds. If he wasn't here, then where was he? Most likely at his house, wondering why I wasn't home to get his return phone call — assuming he felt like calling me back.

What an idiot I was. It was just like David had

said. It would be suicide to try to get down there, suicide. I'd wasted enough time. He just hadn't gone to school today because of what happened last night, and maybe because he didn't want to sit with Lisa at lunch on the day of the dance. I didn't blame him for wanting some time away. I'd find him this weekend, maybe tomorrow, and we'd talk — or not talk, but spend time together. But now I had to get going or I'd be late getting ready for tonight. As I started to trudge back up to the top, I took one more backward glance down the trail.

"Pretty stupid!" I said to myself and shook my head.

Then my eye caught a glimmer of light from the setting sun being reflected up at me from below. I froze in place. I moved my head around to try to recapture the spark of light. Another burst caught my eye. So what? It could be a broken piece of glass, or a pop can, or a shiny stone, or a part that had fallen off a bike . . . or the metal of a wheelchair.

I strained my eyes. Whatever it was, it was hidden behind a large clump of bushes. It was more than two-thirds of the way down. I moved to one side, and then the other, but couldn't see around those bushes. If I wanted to see I'd have to get closer, maybe all the way down there. I glanced at my watch and then at the quickly setting sun. There wasn't much time left before it would get dark, and I knew I couldn't count on any light finding its way down there, far from the street. Either I went down now, and fast, or I'd be coming back up in the dark.

Coming back from what? Finding a piece of metal? Getting home to find out that David had called and that I was a complete idiot? I almost had myself convinced to leave right then when another glitter of reflected light jumped up at me.

I started down the trail. Pebbles and gravel and stones slid down the slope under my shoes. I skidded to a stop and the little landslide continued down another two dozen feet. Not only was it steep, but it was unstable. There was no way anybody could get a wheelchair down this section. Even if he came this far, he would have had to turn back . . . if he could. Once he hit this section, he would have kept on sliding down whether he wanted to stop or not. And if he did slide down, there was no possible way he could have got back up.

I continued on. Soon the trail flattened out, then cut sharply to the left and narrowed. On the one side was a dramatic drop-off that instinctively caused me to move to the other side of the path. This path was hardly wide enough to allow a chair to pass by — or maybe it wasn't. I needed to look over the side.

Without moving any closer, I tried to peer over the edge. It didn't work. I could see farther, but not down to the very bottom — and if he had tipped over the edge, that's where he'd be. I grabbed onto an exposed tree root sticking out of the slope above me. I gave it a pull and it remained firmly in the ground. With one hand tightly gripping the root, I stepped closer and looked over. My knees buckled at the sight of the bottom far below, and I drew myself back quickly without seeing anything. I'd have to look again. I took a deep breath, grabbed the root even tighter, braced my legs, and leaned over the side again. It was a long, sloping drop with jutting rocks and clumps of stunted bushes and a few trees sticking out at awkward angles. I scanned the trail. There was nothing directly below me — thank goodness. I looked farther along the path, trying to find the spot where I'd seen the sparkle of light. I followed the path until my eyes reached the clump of bushes I'd seen before. I still couldn't see anything. Then something moved amongst the leaves. As I watched, David emerged from the other side.

Chapter 23

Spellbound, I watched as he slowly rolled down the path. I wanted to call out to him . . . yell and wave . . . but I didn't. Even if I could dredge out the words, I wasn't sure what they should be. How would I even explain why I was here? I had to get closer . . . maybe by the time I reached his side the words would come.

I released my grip on the root and started down the path. I kept my eyes fixed on David as I moved. He was far away but I could tell there was something wrong about his motion. He seemed to be sort of "limping," or wobbling, as he rolled. I stumbled and sent a shower of stones down the slope. I tried to see if David had noticed, but he'd turned a corner and wasn't visible anymore.

Now that I'd found him, it seemed important

not to let him out of my sight. I kept my eyes on the path and doubled my pace. Suddenly, the slope steepened, and I felt myself speeding down it on the verge of losing control. I rushed around a corner and skidded to a sudden stop as I almost bashed into David. He'd traveled less than a dozen feet since rounding the corner.

Eyes wide and mouth open, his expression mirrored my own shock. Then his features twisted into anger. One whole side of his face was cut and scraped, and dried blood covered part of it. More blood was still flowing from somewhere under his scalp.

"What are you doing here?" David demanded.

"Nothing . . . I was just looking for you . . . you weren't in school today."

"Yeah, so? Who made you the truant officer?"

"Nobody. I was just worried," I stammered.

"Yeah, right," he snapped. "Well, now that you've found me, you can shove off."

"But, your face . . . your head."

He raised a hand to touch his head. His hand was even more scraped and bleeding than his face. "Big deal, I fell."

"You shouldn't have even tried to come down here. It's too dangerous."

"Now you sound like you think you're my mother." He paused. "How did you know to look for me here?"

"Because of what you said the other day."

"What did I say?"

"That you like to come this way to think." Of course, that was only part of what he'd said. I didn't mention the word "suicide."

I looked squarely at him and he looked away. It was then that I noticed the way he was sitting. His chair wasn't pointed down the trail, but aimed straight off the edge. Down below was a drop of over thirty feet onto rocks, jutting out of the river. He had just been sitting there, staring out.

"This is more than just being careless or reckless . . . isn't it?" I questioned.

He didn't answer.

"I understand," I said.

David looked up at me. "You what?"

"I understand," I repeated softly.

"You understand?" he asked in a tone that couldn't disguise his disbelief. "You spend one day in a chair and you think you understand! You think you understand what it's like to be a cripple? To wake up every morning knowing that you're never going to walk again? To have to go to the washroom in a bag?"

I shook my head. "I don't understand that stuff," I mumbled. "Only somebody who's gone through what you went through could know what it's like."

"Then what is it that you think you *do* understand?" he demanded.

"How none of this is fair. How angry I'd be if life did this to me and how I'd want to strike out at anything, or anybody, who got too close."

David snarled. "You don't know me at all!"

"Maybe you're right," I admitted. "Maybe I don't know you at all." I paused. "I thought you were just about the strongest and bravest person I'd ever met. Nothing scared you and nothing stopped you . . ."

He shook his head slowly. "I'm just . . . just tired. Tired of being in this chair, tired of having to deal with everybody . . . prove myself all the time . . . just tired of it all."

"And you want to give up," I said.

He didn't answer.

"Isn't that what you were thinking about when you were staring down at those rocks?"

"You don't know what I was thinking!" he exploded. "What do you think you are, some stupid psychiatrist?" he yelled. "Go away and leave me alone!"

He was on the verge of striking out at me. I wasn't going to fight him. But I wasn't going to go away, either.

"No," I said softly. "The only thing I'm trying to be . . . is your friend."

"I . . . I . . ." he stammered, and I could tell he was trying his hardest to fight back the tears. He slumped forward in his seat and began to sob.

I stepped forward and wrapped my arms around his shoulders. "And I'm not going to let you give up."

Chapter 24

A horn tooted and I pushed aside the curtains to make sure it was David and his father. Their car was at the curb right in front of the house. The horn blared again.

"They're here to get me," I yelled out to my parents. "I'll see you later!"

My mother came out of the kitchen, drying her hands on a dish towel. "How late did you say you'd be?"

"I'm not exactly sure when it'll be over, but the game starts in an hour so it won't be too late," I answered as I pulled on my jacket.

"Who's playing?"

"I'm not even sure. David didn't mention it."

"Do you need any money?" Mom asked.

"Well . . . a few bucks would be nice."

Mom passed me a couple of folded-up bills, which I slipped in my pocket. She reached over and gave me a little kiss on the side of my face. The horn sounded for a third time, louder and longer.

"I better get going." I rushed out the door, jumped down the steps, and ran to the car. I opened the back door and climbed in beside David.

"What took you so long?" David demanded. "I thought we were going to have to leave without you."

"What's the rush?" I asked.

"I don't want to be late."

"We've got a long time before tip-off. Is it far from here?" I asked.

"Not far. It's about a fifteen-minute drive," Tiny answered.

"Then what's the problem? We have plenty of time."

"I just want to get there early," David said.

"Well, I hope your schedule can handle a short stop," his father said.

"A stop for what?"

"Gas. I'm practically running on fumes," he answered as he turned the car into a gas station. "I'll move as fast as I can," he said as he got out of the car.

"Hurry!" David yelled as his father slammed the door shut. He turned to me. "I heard it was a good loss last night."

"How can a loss be good?" I asked in disbelief.

"You know what I mean. You didn't lose by much and I heard you played a good game."

"Who told you that?"

"You, at lunch today," he laughed.

Things had almost gotten back to normal at lunch. Maybe David wasn't quite as friendly to Lisa as he once was. I guess it didn't hurt that he'd taken out another girl — a grade eight — a couple of times.

"Besides me, who told you I played good?" I asked.

"The coach mentioned it to me. He wanted to know why I wasn't in the stands."

"Did you tell him?" I questioned.

"Just told him I had an appointment."

David had been going to see a social worker at the rehabilitation center after school a couple of times a week for the past four weeks. He'd told me about it, but asked that I didn't tell anybody else. That was no problem. Of course, I didn't mention it to anybody — just like I didn't tell anybody about what had happened down in the gorge. That was just between me and him. As far as his parents were concerned, he'd just tripped out of his chair that day as he was coming home from school. I don't think they believed that he could get that injured just from a fall off the curb, but once he agreed to start seeing somebody at the rehab center, they stopped questioning.

"How are things going . . . you know . . . at the center."

"Okay, I guess. Yesterday was my first day in group."

"Group?"

"Yeah, group. It wasn't just the social worker, but a group of kids like me."

"Now that's a scary thought," I said.

"What's so scary about a group of kids in wheelchairs?" David demanded.

"Oh, you meant you were similar because of the chairs," I said. "I thought they were like you in other ways, and one person like you in the world is enough," I laughed as I leaned away from David, thinking he might take a swap at me.

Tiny climbed back in the car. "Fast enough for you?"

David looked at his watch. "Not nearly fast enough. See if you can make up for it by driving dangerously."

"We'll be there in plenty of time. There's nothing to be nervous about."

"I'm not nervous!" David protested. "I just want to make sure the seats are good, right by the court."

"Don't worry," Tiny said.

"Just get me there on time," David replied.

"It's only a few more minutes. Keep your shirt on," Tiny replied. "How's your team doing, Sean?"

"We've won a couple of games," I said "We're

coming along."

"If you ever have a game on a Thursday, let me know. I'd like to drop in and watch," Tiny said.

"That would be nice."

"Here we are," Tiny said. He pulled the car off to the side, turned off the engine, and got out. He then went around to get David's chair. David opened up his door and swung his legs out the side. He pulled himself into the waiting chair and I climbed out after him.

"Wow!" I exclaimed. David was sitting in a brand-new chair.

"When did you get that?"

"A couple of days ago. Pretty neat, huh?"

"That's for sure. It's really different. Where are the arm rests?"

"It doesn't have arms and the back is low. Check out the wheels. They're air filled!"

"Those must make for a smoother ride."

"You're right there. Maybe I'll let you try it out sometime. I'll meet you two inside. There's no ramp at the front doors. I have to go around to the side."

"We'll come with you," I suggested.

"It's faster for you to go through the front and me to wheel around to the side. I want to make sure you get really good seats. Try to get courtside, right by the center. I'll see you inside," David said and turned and scooted away, dodging between the people moving along the sidewalk toward the entrance.

"He really does move fast," I commented.

"Wait and see," Tiny said. "Come on, let's grab a dog and a drink before we sit down."

"Shouldn't we get to our seats?" I questioned. "We don't want David to beat us inside."

"He's moving fast, but we'll get there before him. I guarantee it."

We entered along with a steady stream of other people. I was afraid all the courtside seats would soon be gone.

"How about I go and get our seats while you get the food?"

"Sounds good. Is one dog enough for you?"

"Sure."

His father plowed effortlessly through the crowd, which parted as he went forward. I followed the signs to the seats through a darkened tunnel with light at the end. I exited into the light and found myself standing in the banked arena. A hardwood floor glistened in the center and racks of basketballs waited to be used. The seats were only starting to be filled, from the bottom up, and I bounded down the stairs to secure a few of the last courtside spots. What I needed was two seats beside an open space, like an aisle, where David could park his spiffy new chair. I took the seat beside the aisle and laid my jacket down on the seat beside it to save it for Tiny.

As I settled into my seat I remembered that I still had no idea who was even playing. I guessed it didn't really matter — there was no such thing as bad basketball. I wouldn't have much time to wait, anyway. The teams would be taking to the court soon for their pre-game warm-ups. That was one of the reasons I didn't mind David wanting us here so early. I even loved watching warm-ups. My favorite sound in the world was the squeaking of shoes cutting against the floor.

I looked up and saw David enter the court from the far side. There must be an elevator leading down to courtside, bypassing the stairs. I stood up and waved, but he didn't wave back . . . hold on . . . that wasn't David, it was somebody else in a chair. He looked a lot like him though, and the chair was almost identical. Then behind him out of the same corridor came another wheelchair, and then another and another. And they were all dressed the same, in gold-colored uniforms!

Then I saw David. He came across the court directly toward me. His smile was even brighter than the shiny uniform he wore. He stopped right in front of me.

"Well, what do you think?" he asked.

"I . . . I . . . you're playing?"

"You sound like you don't believe I'm good enough to make a team."

"Of course, I know you can make any team, but why didn't you just tell me?"

"I wanted it to be a surprise. Now that you're surprised, I'm going to put on a show for you.

Maybe you'll see how that sorry team of yours should play."

"I'd like to see that . . . a lot."

"I better join my team for warm-ups. Make sure I can hear you cheering."

"Count on it."

He started away across the floor, then spun, and came back to me. "I forgot. This is for you," he said. He pulled something out from the side of his seat and handed it to me. It was a drawing of David, holding a basketball, wearing his gold uniform, number 99 on the front, a big smile on his face, and the perfect likeness of his fancy chair, with one exception: the wheels had been replaced by basketballs.

"Do you like it?" he asked.

"It's great, but I didn't think you drew pictures of yourself."

"I didn't . . . but things change." He flashed a smile. "You know, Sean, I'm not giving up on anything. Not the hopes I have of getting out of this chair in the future and not the things I can still do while I'm waiting. It's like I said, it isn't what you do with the shots you make, but the ones that don't go in. The rebounds. Do you understand?"

I nodded.

He smiled. "I thought you might."

He turned and headed off to play, and I knew that no matter what the score, the important thing was that David was back in the game.

Eric Walters and I met through a mutual contact a little over two years ago. Since that time, Eric and I have discussed this book and its realism. Being a person who is in a wheelchair, I found that David's experiences in this book are similar to my own.

Also, one of the things that I found about Eric was that he was committed to making his book as factual as possible. In order to do this, Eric accompanied me around my hometown of Milton to see how people reacted, and how difficult or easy it was to physically get around. To get the full effect, Eric used one of my spare wheelchairs and traveled with me through the town, just like Sean and David did. During our excursion, Eric and I both learned a great deal. Eric learned what the abilities of individuals with disabilities are, and got an understanding of how society reacts to people with disabilities. On the other hand, I became more aware of myself, because reading this book, and concentrating on how people reacted to Eric was a reminder of how the greatest disability is attitude.

If you want to find out more about the abilities of individuals with disabilities, you can contact the LINK Foundation at 905-875-LINK (5465) or toll free at 1-800-399-8521. The LINK Foundation was developed to create awareness and opportunities to include the disabled in community sports, fitness, and recreation. The purpose of the LINK Foundation is to facilitate the creation of an information and support network beyond that of a provincial and national sports organization for the disabled. This network serves to increase and promote active living through inclusion at the grass-roots level within families, the education system, communities, and facilities.

Ryan Leworthy,
Co-founder of LINKS